MURDER IN MIND

by

Cheryl Bradshaw

Cover Design © 2014 Indie Designz
Interior book design by
Bob Houston eBook Formatting

ISBN: 1499688954
ISBN-13: 978-1499688955

FOR UPDATES ON
CHERYL AND HER BOOKS

Blog: cherylbradshawbooks.blogspot.com

Web: cherylbradshaw.com

Facebook: Cheryl Bradshaw Books

Twitter: @cherylbradshaw

ALSO BY CHERYL BRADSHAW

Black Diamond Death (Sloane Monroe Series #1)

I Have a Secret (Sloane Monroe Series #3)

Sloane Monroe Series Boxed Set (Books 1–3)

Whispers of Murder (A Novella)

*The first chapters of all Cheryl Bradshaw's books
can be read on her blog*

DEDICATION

This book is dedicated to anyone who's ever had a
dream.
We have but one life, and one opportunity to live it.
Make it last, make it count, and make it the best it can be.
Live your dreams, I know I am.

What kills a skunk is the publicity it gives itself.

-ABRAHAM LINCOLN

CHAPTER 1

Sam Reids reclined back into the seat of his black 1970 Oldsmobile Cutlass Supreme and examined the women that shuffled in and out of the supermarket like predictable herds of cattle. It had been three long years since he felt the steady churn of butterflies in his stomach, but the anticipation of the night's soon-to-be events made it all worthwhile. The wait hadn't been easy, and whenever he felt he couldn't control his urges any longer, he walked down the steep series of steps that led to the basement and gazed at the trinkets he'd collected. They were all spaced two inches apart in single-file formation on a shelf. In total, there were fifteen glass bottles. Each container had a white label about the size of a Post-It note affixed to the front with the date and a name written in thick black marker.

Over the past few years Sam visited them often and took special care to dust and polish their exteriors, but he never opened them once they'd been sealed. He didn't want to take a chance that one of his precious mementos could get spoiled. Sometimes he took one to his room and deposited it on the stand next to him while he slept. When he woke during the night to the illuminated glow that shone through the glass from the lamp above, he felt a sensation of peace, like a child that watched the constant spin of the mobile over the crib. It wasn't the same thrill he'd experienced when he secured the object within the bottle, but it helped him pass the time.

Through his binoculars, Sam observed two women walk out of the store together; one carried a brown paper sack in her hand and the other, a gallon of milk. The one with the sack showed promise. Her long espresso-colored hair flickered in the wind. It reminded him of flames from a forest fire fighting its way across acres of trees. He waited for her to say goodbye to her friend and then placed his binoculars on the seat next to him. His palms expelled an oily substance that spread until they were both drenched with sweat. The time had come.

Sam grabbed an unused diaper from the passenger seat and pushed his car door open. At the same time, the woman unlocked her passenger-side door and bent down and placed the sack of groceries on the seat of her car. She was too preoccupied to hear him approach.

"Excuse me," he said.

The woman retracted out of the car and turned and

faced him.

"Do I know you?" she said.

"I'm sorry to bother you," he said with a crooked smile, "but do you know how to change a diaper?"

She looked at the diaper in his hand and then back at him.

"Why do you ask?"

"My sister asked me to watch my nephew for a few hours, and I can't seem to get the darn thing on right."

He angled the diaper in the direction of his car.

"I'm parked right over there," he said. "Do you think you could help me?"

The woman hesitated and studied the man's car for a moment and then shrugged her shoulders.

"I really need to get home," she said.

The man smiled, but not just any smile. It was one he'd practiced in the mirror over and over again until it conveyed what he needed it to: trust me.

"It will only take a minute," he said.

They walked over to Sam's car, and he was careful to remain a few paces behind her. He glanced over his left shoulder and then his right. All was still, and since the store closed in five minutes, he was certain it would remain that way. He watched the woman peek through the window of his car and relished the startled look on her face when she didn't see a baby. With a perplexed look, she turned and faced him.

"Where's the—"

The man reached into the front pocket of his hoodie with all the calmness of a drug addict who'd just smoked a bag of weed and pulled out a needle and inserted it into her shoulder. In an instant her body went limp and she sagged into him.

Happy anniversary, he thought.

*****

When he arrived home, Sam pulled the woman out of the trunk of his car and placed his hands in the small of her back and tossed her over his right shoulder. Her exposed thigh pressed against the flesh on his face, and he felt her body quiver. It made him feel alive again. The way she looked at him when he opened the trunk and gazed down on her reminded him of a fawn, but she didn't move or make a sound. He was a little disappointed by this; he'd expected more of a challenge.

Sam opened the door to the basement, hauled the woman downstairs, and walked past his bottle collection. For the first time since she'd regained consciousness, the woman tried to scream, but it was muffled by the tape he'd secured over her mouth. He stopped for a moment and turned toward the shelves and patted the side of her leg.

"They're beautiful, aren't they?" he said. "Do you see the row there at the bottom? There's nothing on it now, but in a week or two, it will be all filled up."

The woman twisted her body and thrashed from side to side and tried to release herself from the tight grip he had on her.

Sam just snickered and said, "That's more like it."

He entered a side room that was adorned with a single motif in mind—plastic, and he laid her body across a white padded board in the center of the room. He secured her into the wrist and ankle restraints and then removed the duct tape from her lips.

"There now," he said, "that's better."

A tear trickled down the side of her face, and he took his finger and brushed it away.

"Now, now. There's no need for that," he said.

"Are you going to kill me?"

He smiled and ran his hand through her hair.

"You have beautiful hair," he said. "It's so soft. So well taken care of; I admire that in a woman."

"Please don't hurt me," she said. "I'll do whatever you want. If you want money, it's yours, and I won't say anything to anyone, I promise."

It was the same plea he'd heard time and time again. The final plea of a terrified woman who'd pledge anything to save herself. He lifted his pointer finger and placed it in the center of her lips.

"Shhh," he said. "I need you to hold still for me. Nod if you understand."

She didn't move.

"I asked you to nod if you understand," he said. "It isn't polite not to respond, especially since you're a guest in my house."

She bobbed her head up and down and another tear escaped from her eyelid.

"This next part is going to hurt for a moment," he said, "but I find it's best to get it over with."

CHAPTER 2

TWO DAYS LATER

I pushed the shower curtain aside and lunged for my cell phone which had been ringing off and on in a consistent pattern for the past several minutes. Whoever it was really wanted to get a hold of me. I checked my phone and had two missed calls—one from Nick and the other from Maddie. They both seemed burdened by something, and Maddie was on her way over, but she wouldn't say why.

I stepped out of the shower and dried off and walked into the living room. A news reel ran across the bottom of my television screen with information about a homicide. I grabbed the remote and jacked the volume up. The female reporter on the screen was situated in front of a grocery store in Kimball Junction. She wore an ill-fitted pastel suit and enough makeup to last her for the rest of the week. The look on her face was grave and told a story all its own.

"This is Kennedy Price reporting from KRD news," she said. *"In the early hours of the morning, a jogger discovered the body of a woman about ten feet from where I stand now. The police haven't released many details, and no names have been made public, but what we can tell you is the victim was a female in her late twenties or early thirties, and it's being reported that she had long, dark hair. Many of our viewers will remember the brutal, sadistic murders of several young women that took place right here in Park City a few short years ago. The killer, who went by the self-proclaimed name Sinnerman, was never caught, which leads us to wonder—"*

She paused a moment and put her finger on the earpiece that was latched to the side of her ear and then continued.

"We've just received word that the victim's name is Phoebe Summers. She was a married mother of two young girls and a long-time Park City resident. From what we've just learned, she had the trademark letter S carved into her wrist, apparently from a knife, police believe. Unless it's some kind of copycat killing, it appears the Sinnerman murders have started up again."

A text popped up on my phone from Maddie:

Almost there, don't turn on the TV, okay? I need to

talk to you first.

It was too late for that.

The news anchor changed to a male with a glossy bald head, and the topic of murder was replaced with a segment on grilling steaks the right way which didn't seem like an appropriate segue after they'd just terrified every brunette alive within an hour radius.

I switched the television off and sat down on the sofa. Lord Berkeley, a.k.a. Boo, woke from his slumber, scooted his furry white body next to me, and propped his head up on my pant leg. I stroked him and thought about Gabby and how long I'd waited for this day to come.

A sound echoed from my front door with an accompanying noise like someone was slapping the palm of their hands against it—repeatedly.

"Sloane, you in there? Open up."

I unlocked the door, yanked it back, and was met with a flushed and tired Maddie, who clung to my door like she'd just sprinted in the 100-yard dash. Her blond hair was in its usual pigtails, and she wore a ribbed, lavender tank top with a white one beneath it and a pair of jean shorts with the insides of the pockets sticking out the bottom. From the look of her, one would never guess she'd been alive for more than three-and-a-half decades.

"I saw the news," I said.

She threw her arms around me and squeezed—hard.

"Are you all right? I've been worried about you all

day."

"I will be once I get more information about the woman who was murdered," I said. "Did they bring her to you?"

She nodded.

"Have you examined her yet?" I said.

"They called me out to the scene when she was discovered."

"So what do you think—is it him?" I said.

"We should talk about this when I have more information. My main concern right now is how you're dealing with all of this."

Maddie and I had known each other for almost twenty years, and over that time I had learned to decipher a lot of things about her, including when she was keeping something from me.

"What aren't you telling me?" I said. "You were the ME on this case the first time around, and I expect you are again, which means if anyone has first-hand knowledge, it's you."

"I want to ask you something; let's say it turns out to be the same sick wacko who murdered your sister a few years ago, what are you going to do?"

"Whatever it takes, you know that," I said. "You've known me long enough to realize I won't stop this time until he's caught. And if you have any information that would help me succeed, I need to know what it is. Don't hold out on me."

We walked over to the couch and sat down. Maddie dug into her Chanel bag, pulled out a piece of gum, and popped it into her mouth. Some people smoke to relieve tension, but not Maddie. Gum was her form of nicotine. She lounged back and propped her hands up behind her head and stared at the ceiling for a moment and then looked over at me and sighed.

"All right, here's what I know. The victim was female and around the same age your sister was when she was taken, give or take a few years. And she was killed in a similar way—she had the same bruises in the shape of fingers on the sides of her neck, and her hyoid bone was fractured."

"What about the method? Was it the same as before?"

She nodded.

"It's the same," she said. "Sinnerman predominately used his right hand to strangle his victims, and the fingerprints on this victim have the same inconsistency. The fingerprints indentations on the right side of her neck are smaller, and there are only three of them, like he only used a few fingers from his left hand. It's something I've never been able to figure out."

"I always assumed he had some kind of deformity," I said. "Did he, umm—"

"Rape her?"

I nodded.

"No."

The more she went on and on about the victim, the more it resembled the other killings.

"Bound?" I said.

"Yep—there were bruises on one of her wrists and both ankles."

"What about the symbol?" I said. "The news reported the deceased woman had knife wounds."

"She had the same three slashes in the shape of an S on her wrist."

"Or more like a backward Z after he carves his signature," I said.

"And she had one gash by her upper thigh that spanned about three inches."

"That's one thing I've never understood. Why a single cut on the leg of one victim and several on another?" I said.

Maddie shrugged.

"There was one difference this time," she said. "He didn't sever all the fingers from one of her hands like he did in the first round of killings; the vic's entire right hand was missing."

"He's becoming more aggressive," I said.

"Or he's a copycat."

I shook my head.

"I don't think so. My guess is that he's bored with the

fingers and needs an even bigger thrill. To slice their fingers off isn't good enough anymore."

Maddie leaned forward and took my hands in hers and rested them on her knee.

"You want to know something?" she said. "I'm proud of you."

"For what?"

"I violated about a hundred traffic laws on my way here, and the whole time, all I could think about was how I was going to break the news to you that this creep could be back. And then I get here, and you're calmer than I am."

"I've had time to deal with it," I said.

"Well, if it's him, we'll know soon enough."

I leaned toward Maddie.

"Oh it's him all right. He's back—and he's killing again."

CHAPTER 3

My front door rattled like a herd of angry elephants were pressed against it.

"What the hell?" Maddie said.

I stood and Maddie shot up from her position on the sofa and stepped in front of me.

"Allow me," she said.

She walked to the door and glanced out the peephole.

"Solicitors?"

"Worse," she said. "Reporters."

"News travels fast."

"How do you want to handle this?" she said.

I walked over to the door.

"If I don't talk to them, they'll just hound me until I do."

She raised her pointer finger in front of my face and wagged it in a swirl pattern.

"Oh-no-you're-not," she said.

"Maddie, I'm fine. I can deal with it."

"So can I," she said.

And with that she twisted the knob on the door and flung it open and then walked out and slammed it behind her. I pulled back the curtain in my front entrance and got ready for the show to begin.

"Listen up, people," Maddie said. "Sloane won't be giving any interviews today or any other day. You've got ten seconds to back the hell off her property or I'll call the cops. Your choice."

The stunned crowd remained unmoved until Maddie began the countdown.

"Nine, eight, seven—"

A male reporter segregated himself from the pack and approached her. His pants were baggy, and he was in serious need of a belt. His t-shirt looked like it'd been used for a napkin—multiple times. He sized her up, snickered, and then turned his palm up, holding it out like a traffic cop who had just initiated a halt in movement.

"Look lady, you can't do nothin', and we don't have to leave," he said. "We've got every right to be here, so why don't you turn your little rah rah buffalo stance around like a good little girl and go back into the house and get Miss Monroe for us, okay?"

He'd just made a big mistake. Maddie yanked her cell phone out of her pocket, pressed some numbers, and spoke loud enough for those who were brave enough to remain to hear.

"Chief Sheppard, this is Madison. I'm at Sloane's, and we've got a situation. A bunch of reporters have blocked her front entrance, and she can't get out. They have also taken to yelling obscenities since she won't come out of her house, and I'm worried about her safety."

The reporter's forehead wrinkled in about five places and he shouted, "What the—you little liar!"

Maddie paid him no mind and continued.

"Thanks, I'll expect them in ten," she said, and then she ended the call and gave the man the Maddie Special—an icy stare with everything on it.

"What's your name?" she said to him.

He failed to respond and instead, he backed out of the driveway in a brisk manner and turned toward the street.

"Your name?" she said, louder. "What is it?!"

He pretended like he didn't hear her and kept on truckin'. She reached in her pants pocket and pulled out a bill and hoisted it into the air.

"Twenty dollars for the person who gives me his name right here, right now."

The remaining crowd scattered like there was a one-hour clearance going on at Macy's and within a matter of seconds most of the onlookers were gone, except for one. She wasn't dressed like the other women in their uptight skirts, suit jackets, and nude nylon stockings with colored pumps that looked like they'd been in their closets since the eighties. She wore a simple, short-sleeved sweater and a pair of jeans and aimed her eyes toward the ground while she spoke.

"His name is Tim Wallace," she said. "Will you tell Miss Monroe I'm sorry if I've upset her by being here?"

Maddie's eyebrows shot up, speechless.

I opened the front door.

"What's your name?" I said.

The reporter looked up at me.

"Kelly Price."

"How long have you been a reporter?"

"This is my first assignment. I don't even have a list of questions really. I just wanted to talk to you. They already have the paper set to run tonight, but I was told if I could get a statement from you of any kind, they'd move things around somehow and put you on the front page. I just have to be back there within the hour."

I motioned with my hand, and she walked over to me.

"Come inside for a minute," I said.

I glanced at Maddie who nodded but stayed in position. I couldn't have asked for a better protector of the realm.

I closed the front door and turned to the reporter.

"Let's sit for a minute," I said.

She walked over and sat on the edge of the sofa, and

I positioned myself in a chair across from her. Lord Berkeley scampered around the corner and, sensing there was an intruder in his midst, brandished a mouthful of clenched teeth.

The reporter folded her arms over her knees and leaned back on the couch.

"Your dog—is he, umm, going to attack me?" she said.

I shook my head.

"He just wants you to know he's aware of your presence." I patted the corner of my chair with my hand. "Come here, Boo."

He hopped up on the chair and rested his head on my thigh, but didn't take his eyes off the intruder.

"Who do you work for?" I said.

"The *Park City Beat*. They wanted me to write an article about your sister so I drove over to talk to you, but I had no idea so many people would be here."

"That's okay," I said. "I'll give you the article you want if you agree to print one thing for me."

She smiled and reached into her shoulder bag, retrieving a pen and a pad of yellow-lined paper.

"Name it."

"To be honest, I'm not interested in an article that rehashes what I went through a few years ago," I said. "I want you to send a message to the killer for me."

Her eyes widened like they'd been propped open

with toothpicks.

"You can't be serious."

"I've never been so sure of anything in my life," I said.

She bobbed her shoulders up and down.

"All right then, what do you want to say—do you want to address him directly?"

I nodded.

"Tell him this: I'm coming for you, and this time, I won't stop until the only life you have left is behind bars."

CHAPTER 4

Maddie left, turning her post over to Nick, who'd entered the house with a displeased look on his face.

"*I'm coming for you?* You're kidding me—right?"

"I hoped Maddie would keep that to herself for now," I said.

He slid his hand into his back pocket and pulled out his cell phone and flipped it open.

"I assume they haven't run the paper yet since that girl was just here a few minutes ago," he said. "One quick call and I can have it taken out."

I shook my head and placed my hand over his phone and pushed it down.

"It stays," I said.

"Are you trying to put a target on your back?"

"If that's what it takes to get his attention, then yes," I said.

"Even if that means you'd put yourself at risk?"

I sighed. He was in one of those moods where it didn't matter what I said. He couldn't be reasoned with, and it almost took more effort than it was worth to try.

"Maybe it would be best if we didn't talk about this right now," I said.

Nick walked over to me and placed both hands on the sides of my shoulders and looked me square in the eye.

"This guy is out there killing women, and he could be anyone. Hell, he could be your next door neighbor for all you know. We don't even have any good leads yet. All you're asking for is trouble."

"I'm asking for justice, and I thought we both wanted that—for Gabby and all the other victims. This creep has gotten away with a slew of murders. He walks free while the women he murdered live in eternal unrest inside a coffin, knowing the man who killed them is still out there. They've been robbed, all of them, from the opportunity of a full life. And if I have even the slightest chance to catch the guy this time and send him straight to hell, I'm going to take it."

"You shouldn't be anywhere near this. You're too emotional. Can't you see that?"

"It's too late for that," I said. "I was involved from the moment he took Gabby from me."

Nick shook his head.

"By the end of the week I bet we have a dozen guys

on this, not to mention the FBI. That's why it would be best for you to let us do our job."

"Don't you mean it would be better for *you*?" I said. "That's what you believe, isn't it? Just because you're a detective doesn't mean you have the right to make decisions for me."

He grimaced and detached his hands from my shoulders, and then walked into the kitchen and grabbed a glass and the bottle of Crown Royal out of the cabinet. He poured himself a drink and took a nice long swig and then hammered it down on the counter. The glass made a ringing sound when it hit and a portion of the liquid flew up into the air and sloshed down on the counter. I wanted to say: *I'm not cleaning that up*, but I didn't.

After a minute of silence where Nick downed the rest of his drink, and I tried not to focus on the liquid that had spread in two directions and trickled like a diminutive stream toward the edge of my counter, he looked over at me and said, "I understand your feelings for the guy, or the lack thereof, and you have every right to hate him for what he's done—no one disputes that. But if you go after him on your own, you'll put yourself at risk and I can't allow that."

He can't allow it?

"Maybe you should go," I said.

"I just got here."

I grabbed my keys off the counter.

"Then I'll go. It's been a long day. I need some time to think."

He started to say something, but it was too late. I was already out the front door, and it had shut itself behind me. And for the first time since Nick appeared, I remembered what it felt like to breathe again.

CHAPTER 5

In the years that had elapsed since Gabrielle's death, not a single day went by when I didn't think of her or him, whoever he was, and though I hated the fact that the killings had resumed, him being back on the prowl gave me the second chance I needed—once again, he was within my grasp. The first time around I was too wrapped up in my emotions with the loss of Gabby to concentrate on catching her killer. I left it to the homicide unit to do that, and I thought they would come through and find the piece of trash responsible for the brutal killings. But they didn't, and I wasn't about to let that happen again. Not this time.

I hopped out of bed and walked to the front door and opened it. The morning sun blasted its rays across my face, and I held my hand in front of my eyes to shield myself from it while I reached down with the other and retrieved the paper. I shut the front door and carried it to the kitchen. Lord Berkeley trotted past me and yawned and then went over to his water bowl and peered in. When he didn't see what he wanted, he stuck one paw in the bowl and moved it back and forth which produced a sound like a quarter being dropped into a glass jar.

"Your mommy is going to be the talk of the town today," I said to him.

He looked at me and then at his bowl and then back at me again. His only concern seemed to be whether what I just said had anything to do with him getting what he wanted, now. I gripped his bowl in my hand and topped it off and set it back down. He did a few spins to show his eternal gratitude and then buried his face in the bowl and savored his reward.

I made some tea and pulled the rubber band off the paper. It fell open, and the headline of the day was revealed for all to see in bold capital letters:

SISTER OF MURDER VICTIM GABRIELLE MONROE VOWS REVENGE!

It was a bit on the dramatic side, but the paper had done its job. The headline was followed by an article that chronicled the events in the order in which they happened three years earlier. The past had come back, and I'd been given a second chance. I leaned back in my chair and smiled. Ready, set—go.

CHAPTER 6

The day was halfway gone when I walked through the double doors of the Park City Police Station. Rose looked up from the reception desk when I entered and grinned.

"Sloane, it's great to see you. I've had you on my mind all day today."

"Good to see you too," I said.

"Are you doing okay?"

It had been less than eighty hours since Sinnerman's latest victim was captured and killed, and the main thing on everyone's mind was how I was dealing with it. I'd started to feel like a wounded puppy—but I put on a brave face and smiled because in the end, I knew they meant well.

"I'm just fine Rose," I said. "I appreciate your concern. Is Coop around?"

She wrinkled her nose and made a face like a foul odor had just wafted into the building.

"For a smart girl, you sure like to take your chances," she said.

I smiled.

"Is he here?"

She pointed in the direction of a side room, which housed computers and the like.

"If you follow the scent of Old Spice, you'll smack right into him," she said.

We both laughed, and I thanked her. She nodded with a crazed look still cemented on her face but said nothing.

Coop was alone when I snuck into the room, and his face was positioned about two inches away from the computer screen. He was eyeballing some photos of women, one of whom was my sister. I stood inside the doorway and knocked on the wall a few times to get his attention. He jerked his head up and swung it around and then pressed a button on the keyboard. The screen went black. He made a barely audible grunt noise and turned his head away from me.

"Nick's not in here," he said.

"Nice to see you too," I said. "I'm not here for him."

Coop and I had a history, and most of it wasn't good. Earlier that year, he'd come to my rescue and I thought we'd reached a turning point in our relationship, but it didn't take long for things to get back to the usual snarky attitude we had for each other. He didn't respect my line of work, and therefore, had little use for me. And no matter how hard I tried to be civilized, I never managed to get my foot in the door long enough to maintain a decent relationship with him either.

"What do you want?"

"I think you know," I said.

He shook his head back and forth.

"I can't talk about the case and you know it, and even if I could, I wouldn't talk to you about it," he said. "Besides, you're the big shot PI. Aren't you supposed to be able to figure this stuff out on your own?"

Back when the killings first started, Coop was lead detective on the case, and I imagine he still lost sleep over the fact that he never caught the elusive Sinnerman. The guy was the only one I'd ever heard of who'd slipped through Coop's elongated fingers. And even though he pretended not to care a stitch about me, I was sure he felt he'd let me down. My sister's killer was still out there, and he could have stopped him, and not only had he failed in his mind, now he had to deal with an even harsher reality: women were dying again. I never held it against him—the whole of the blame resided with one individual, Sinnerman himself, and there wasn't anything anyone could have done. If there was one thing I knew about Coop, it was that there wasn't a detective on the planet who worked harder than he did.

"Has he made contact with you yet?" I said.

"What makes you think he will?"

"Because he did before. You were the only one he communicated with a few years ago. And I figured since he chose you the first time, there's no reason he wouldn't do it again."

"Maybe he has, maybe he hasn't."

I started to wonder what the hell I was thinking trying to communicate to him at all.

The sound of papers shuffled behind me.

I circled around and saw Nick who had inhabited the space surrounding the copy machine in the corner of the room. He had a stack of papers in his hand, like he needed to make some copies, but he didn't—he just stood there. "What are you two talking about?" he said.

"Nothing," Coop and I both said in unison.

"If that's truc, there's no need to stop just because I'm here."

The interesting thing about his comment was that I had a hunch Nick saw me enter the room and found a reason to come in after me so he would know what I was up to.

Coop stood up from his chair. "She was just leaving," he said.

Coop had the height of a basketball player and was the size of a pro wrestler, which wasn't bad for someone old enough to be my father.

"I wasn't finished with my questions," I said.

"I was," Coop said, and he exited the room.

"What did you think you were going to get out of him by coming here?" Nick said.

"Has Sinnerman communicated with him yet?"

"I'm not talking to you about that," Nick said.

"So we're just going to act like none of this is happening, is that it?"

"If it keeps you safe, yes. The less you know, the better."

"There isn't a thing you can do to keep me away from this," I said.

Nick wadded up the papers and threw them across the room. They collided with the wall and single sheets fluttered through the air. I wasn't sure what he was going for, but I assumed it was dramatic effect.

"If you want to nose around, I can't stop you," he said, "but you won't get any information out of me—not now, not ever. I meant what I said last night. I don't want you involved in this, and if that means you're mad at me, I guess that's how it is. And don't bother going to anyone else around here because they won't talk to you either."

I wasn't mad, I was disappointed. It had only been a few months since we moved in together as a couple—after he insisted we take our relationship to the next level or it was over—

and we'd been doing fine until he decided to get involved with the cases I took. No case was simple enough that

Nick didn't discourage me from taking it, and the constant bickering about what I was doing and where I was going all the time had taken its toll on me. For us to work, I needed him to support me and not micromanage my every move. I was beginning to think that wasn't possible.

Nick seemed aware that I was in deep contemplation.

"This is for the best, Sloane," he said. "It really is. You might not see that now, but you will, and then you'll thank me for it."

I doubted that.

I shrugged him off and exited the police station. Halfway to my car, I picked up my cell phone and pressed number two on my speed dial.

"Maddie, it's me. Can you break for lunch? I need you."

She popped a bubble into the phone and laughed.

"Sure thing," she said. "Just tell me when and where and I'll be there."

My eyes flashed on a piece of pastel pink paper that was creased in half under my windshield wiper. I leaned over the hood and grabbed it. My first instinct was that it was an advertisement of some sort. I was about to crunch it up in my hand when I noticed it wasn't what I'd thought at all.

"Hold on a second Maddie," I said.

"Make it quick. The little girl's room is calling my

name."

I situated my keys and my phone on top of my car and opened the note. A series of words in all caps was scrawled in a diagonal pattern across the page in red pen that slanted upward from left to right on three lines:

HELLO SLOANE MONROE
SINNERMAN HERE
LET'S PLAY

My stomach lurched, and I felt like I'd eaten a bowl full of rocks for breakfast followed by a large glass of milk that had gone sour. I dropped to my knees and squatted next to my car, while I pivoted around and canvassed the area, but I saw no one. No cars out of place and no people, anywhere.

I took my phone in my hand.

"Maddie, are you still there?" I said, in a whisper.

"Sure am. You gonna tell me what's going on, or what?"

"I need to call you back."

CHAPTER 7

I folded the note and tucked it inside my bag and wondered if Sinnerman was off somewhere not far away with his eyes held fast on me at that very moment. If he was, I didn't want him to sense the twisted knot that wrenched my insides. I slung my bag over my shoulder and fought off the urge to race back to the police station. *Just put one foot in front of the other and take it slow*, I told myself, *and breathe*. You can do this.

Rose raised an eyebrow when she saw that I'd returned.

"You're not back for another round with Coop again, I hope," she said.

I shook my head.

"Is the chief around?"

She spun her chair to the right and leaned over and stretched her neck out like an ostrich and stared down the hall.

"I can just make out the top of his head," she said. "Looks like he's in his office. Do you want me to—"

I shook my head.

"That's okay; I'll let him know I'm here."

Nick was seated at his desk engrossed in some sort of silly war game on his computer when I went by, and thankfully, he didn't notice me. I entered through the open door of the chief's office and tried to be discreet while I sealed it shut behind me. The chief had his cell phone fastened to his ear, and his eyes were honed in on something out his office window. He swung around and caught sight of me and made a swift motion with his finger to keep me quiet while he finished his call. I moved to the chair in front of his desk and sat and waited.

"Look," he said into his phone. "I don't care what you have to do—I want answers and I want them now. Call me back when you've got something, and until you do, there's no reason to have this conversation. You got me?!"

He slammed the phone down, took a deep breath in, let out an exasperated sigh, and then shoved the mess of papers to the side of his desk. He curved his body forward. I hesitated. He wasn't in the best mood, and the last thing I wanted was to make it worse, but there was no getting around it.

"Do you have a few minutes?" I said.

His eyes darted in my direction.

"You wanna know something, kiddo?" he said, "I knew you'd pop up in my office today. And here you are."

I stretched my hand inside my bag and felt the slip of paper. Out of the corner of my eye I caught a glimpse of Nick who had just discovered I was back in the station and perched inside the chief's office. He shot up out of his chair like he was a pilot aboard Apollo 13 who had just been cleared for takeoff and sprinted for the door.

"Listen," I said to the chief, in a hushed tone, "I need to talk to you about something—alone. It's important."

The chief, who by this time had also observed Nick's speedy approach, shook his head and ran one of his hands through his overgrown mustache.

"I'm not the playground monitor," he said, "and this isn't preschool, Sloane. If you two are having problems, you need to sort that out on your own."

"Please," I said.

It was the only word I could get out before Nick landed at the door, opened it, and shuffled in. He glared at me and then the chief.

"What's she doing in here with you?" Nick said.

"You ever heard of knocking, Calhoun?" the chief said. "Last time I checked this was *my* office."

"And she's *my* business."

In all the years that I'd known the chief, I'd never seen his body move at the rate it did in that moment. It was like seeing a scene from a movie play out in fast forward. He nabbed Nick's arm and with one push, forced him out the door he'd just come through.

"I'll be right back," the chief said over his shoulder.

And with that, the two of them walked in a brisk manner down the hall and out of sight. A few minutes later, the chief returned, but Nick was nowhere in sight.

"Everything all right?" I said.

"It is now that I've given the boy the rest of the day off."

"Sorry about that."

The chief pulled out the chair behind his desk and lowered himself into it.

"That boyfriend of yours is quite the hothead sometimes," he said. "I thought he had more respect for you than that."

"He's just been on edge. It's complicated," I said.

With Nick off the premises, I pulled my hand back out of my bag and dispensed the note onto the chief's desk and said, "The reason why I'm here is because of this."

He snatched it up and scrutinized both sides and then shrugged.

"What's this supposed to be then?"

"Read it," I said.

He unfolded it, read it in silence, and then looked over at the unadorned wall to the right and repeated the words on the paper several times out loud.

"Is this what I think it is?"

I nodded.

"You can add he reads the local paper to his profile," I said.

"When did you get this, and how?"

"About fifteen minutes ago, I went to leave the station, and it was under the windshield on my car," I said.

"In *my* parking lot?"

I nodded.

The chief opened his desk drawer and pulled out a piece of plastic and deposited the note inside.

"The nerve of this guy," he said. "Unbelievable."

He turned toward me.

"And you," he said. "What the hell were you thinking with that newspaper article anyway?"

"At the time, all that mattered to me was getting his attention."

He placed his fingers on the pressure points of both sides of his forehead and squeezed.

"Well, you succeeded."

"Has he made contact with Coop yet?" I said.

The chief placed his finger on the center of the plastic that held the note.

"This is the first we've heard from him since the murders started up again."

"That's about what I expected," I said.

He squinted his eyes.

"What's that supposed to mean?"

"I'm just not shocked he hasn't contacted him, that's all," I said.

"Should I be concerned about what you're not saying with that statement?"

"Let me ask you a question," I said.

He shrugged.

"Shoot."

"That phone call you were on just now—were you trying to find out who leaked the news to the press?" I said.

"Why does that matter to you?"

"Because no one in this office betrayed you if that's what you think happened," I said.

"And you know this because…?"

"Call it female intuition," I said. "I've spent enough time thinking about this guy and how he works."

"Yeah well, you're not the only one." He sat quiet for a time and then said, "Let's say I believe your theory, and I'm not saying I do—but if it didn't come from my men, who then?"

I pointed to the pink slip of paper.

"He did it."

"Sinnerman?"

I nodded.

"It's important to him that the press gets the information right, and he wants everyone to know what happened. If you won't release it, he'll do it himself. It's that simple."

"You know I can't keep this note from Nick," he said. "My entire department will be privy to it before long."

"I know," I said. "I just didn't want to be here when Nick found out whose car that thing was left on. I have enough to deal with right now."

"Are things that bad between you two?"

I stood up and pushed my chair in.

"To be honest, I don't know what they are anymore," I said.

"Well, it looks like this Sinnerman, or whatever he's calling himself these days, is back to his old ways," the chief said. He picked up the plastic bag that contained the note and jiggled it in the air. "You know what this means, don't you?"

"We've just increased our chances of catching him?" I said.

He shook his head.

"It means I can't have you out there on your own."

"Why not? I'll be fine. I always have—this isn't any different."

"I didn't ask for your opinion, Sloane. I'll assign a detail to keep an eye on you from here on out. And before you open your mouth in protest, you should know it isn't up for debate. I'm putting one of my best guys on you, and that's final."

CHAPTER 8

Maddie and I sat on a bench at Rotary Park. She half-listened to what I had to say and the rest of the time peered over her shoulder. When she couldn't keep quiet any longer she said, "Who's the hottie at four o'clock?"

"I've named him."

"What?"

I nodded.

"Taye Diggs," I said.

He shared the height of the real Taye Diggs, but had twice the muscle—maybe even three times.

"You don't know his real name?" she said.

"All I've been able to get out of him so far is that he's been assigned to me. I tried to strike up a rapport, but he wasn't interested. I dare you to say something to him. We'll see if he grunts at you too."

"A guy who doesn't want to spend all day playing mad gab with a woman—whoever heard of such a thing?" she said.

We both laughed.

"Well sweetie, I hope this is what you wanted," she said, "because there's no going back now."

"It's not so bad," I said. "So I have a muscular shadow for a while. It could be worse."

"That's not what I meant," she said. "Who knows what this freak knows about you—where you live, where you work." She put her hand on my shoulder. "Promise me you'll be careful."

"He could have found all that information without my public announcement," I said. "I just sped up the process for him."

Maddie took a sip of her blue raspberry Slurpee.

"Yep, and that's a nice target you've attached to your backside."

"I'll be fine," I said.

"That note he left you has me all kinds of freaked out," she said. "Nick is gonna flip when he finds out. Have you heard from him?"

I shook my head.

"I don't know Maddie. Things with us are...well...not how I thought they were going to be."

"I'm sorry," she said.

"What do you have to apologize for?"

"Everything. I feel like I pushed you into moving in together," she said. "You didn't think you were ready, and

I saw how happy you were, or seemed to be, and told you to go for it, and now you have, and—"

"You didn't force me into anything. I'm a big girl, and I made my own decision. I just didn't know it was going to be like this."

She took another gulp of her Slurpee except it was just about gone, and all she seemed to suck up through her straw was ten percent Slurpee and a bunch of air. I snatched the cup from her and set it on the ground next to me for safe keeping.

"I'm pretty sure you're done with this," I said.

"Can I tell you something?"

"Anything."

"You seem different now that the two of you are living together."

"When we moved in, he changed," I said. "Sometimes I feel like I'm living in the movie *Far and Away*, and he's just been given the deed to my life and has staked his claim on me like I'm his property and he holds all the rights to it."

"I'm glad you're getting it out," she said. "I've wanted to talk to you about it for a while now. The dude's a total control freak. I used to like him, but now—I don't like what I see."

"I know," I said. "I don't either."

"What are you gonna do?"

I shrugged.

"I need some time to think about it," I said. "And right now, it's too much for me to deal with. I need to focus on Sinnerman."

She nodded.

"Listen, not to change the subject, but I wondered if you'd mind if I brought a date tomorrow to dinner?"

"You don't have to ask my permission," I said. "Bring whoever you want."

"Yes, well, about that—"

"Oh don't tell me you made a date with Taye Diggs in the short amount of time we've been here."

She laughed.

"Not him, but he is someone you know."

Of the two of us, Maddie was the outspoken one more often than not, but at that moment, her hesitation spoke volumes.

"What's with all the secrecy?" I said. "Out with it."

"Okay then, it's Wade."

"Wade?"

She swerved her body to the side and bumped her shoulder on mine.

"You know," she said.

I was confused. Had I missed something? I sat there and tried to think of anyone I'd ever known named Wade. And then it dawned on me.

"Do you mean to say your date is with Chief Sheppard?"

I couldn't remember the last time anyone around me referred to him by his first name.

"The one and only," she said.

"Wow, you and the chief. I never would have thought—"

"I know, isn't it great?!"

CHAPTER 9

I woke the next morning and rolled over and tried to make out the numbers displayed on the clock that hung over my closet door. It was time to climb out of bed, but all I wanted was to pull the covers over me and return to the depths of my slumber. I should have embraced the day with happiness, but glee was the farthest thing from my mind. It was my birthday, the one day a year to celebrate my existence in the world, but I could never get through it without thinking of Gabby and all the memories we missed out on together because she wasn't here.

I wondered if other people felt the same way I did after their loved ones died and what I would change if I could go back in time and be with her again if I knew what was to come. I would have talked to her more often and not just once a week like we were obligated to form some regular contact because we were sisters. Now I wished I'd spoken to her every day and planned more trips with her and let her know how much she meant to me. I should have shouted my love for her from the rooftops, and I was ashamed I thought about all those things now when I couldn't do any of it. It didn't seem right to me that so many people in the world waited too long to express their feelings to their loved ones, and yet that's exactly what I'd done with Gabby.

After she died, I found myself at confession airing out all my regrets to the local priest, even though I hadn't been to church for years. The priest in all of his infinite wisdom told me I shouldn't concern myself over such things and said Gabby was in a better place now, and she knew how I felt. He said one day we would be together again. But would we—how could he be so sure?

Lord Berkeley hopped up on the bottom of the bed and scampered across the blanket until he was about an inch in front of my face. He looked out the window and then at me and made a noise that sounded like he needed some cheese to go along with his whine.

"All right, Boo," I said, "time to get up."

I swept him up in my arms, attached his leash, and opened the front door. Taye Diggs was hunkered down on one of my lawn chairs with his eyes fixated on the street in front of my house.

"Morning," I said.

He glanced at me for a second and lifted his chin a

few inches, but otherwise didn't respond. He was dressed in a different color shirt, which meant at some time he must have left and someone else took the shift for the night, but who that was—I couldn't say. Nick had slept on the couch all night and left hours earlier. It was just a matter of time before he ruptured over the note.

I walked Lord Berkeley around the cul-de-sac and my loyal protector hung back about twenty paces behind me. It made me feel a little bit like a celebrity with my own personal bodyguard, and I wondered if I kept going around if he would continue to walk in circles with me. I imagined he would, and it might have been fun to test it out, but I decided not to push it.

When Lord Berkeley had his exercise for the morning, I reentered the house and made some breakfast and then leaned my body halfway out the front door and invited Taye inside. He frowned at me like I was out of my mind and shook his head. I returned to the kitchen, grabbed the two plates I'd made up, walked outside and plopped down in the adjoining chair across from him.

"Well," I said, "if you won't come in, I guess I'll come out."

He looked off to the side at nothing, let out a long exaggerated sigh, and then faced me.

"I have a job to do. And all this," he said and pointed to the food, "it's a distraction."

"It's eggs and toast," I said. "You have to eat, right?"

I held the plate out and wiggled it a few inches from his nostrils in an attempt to rouse his appetite, and for the first time since we'd met, he cracked a smile. It was slight and barely noticeable to the untrained eye, but there nonetheless. It may not have been a mouthful of bright whites, but it was a start.

"I'll eat this, lady, but then you have to go back inside, okay?"

"I can live with that," I said.

We sat across from one another and ate our food in silence. I was leery about whether I should engage him in a verbal exchange he didn't want to have, so I tried my best to act like it felt natural to sit there and remain mute. Taye managed to shovel gargantuan-sized spoonfuls of eggs into his mouth without the slightest glance toward his plate, which fascinated me enough to endure the silence. While he chewed, his eyes darted around to the street, the side yard, the bushes, and then back to the street again.

A car turned up the road and steered its way in the direction of my humble abode. Taye didn't miss a beat. He shoved his plate into my lap and stuck his hand under the side of his shirt and placed it on his waist and rested it there. The few inches of skin he exposed revealed a six pack, the likes of which I'd only seen in the movies, and I couldn't peel my eyes away from it.

"You should go back inside," he said. "Now."

I arched my body over the side of my chair and stared out into the street.

"It's just Nick," I said.

He squinted and rose from his chair to get a better look.

"Detective Calhoun?"

I nodded.

"Wonder what he's doing here," he said.

"He, uh, lives here," I said.

Taye Diggs twisted his face into a shape that reminded me of one of those apples that people let sit forever, and then when they were good and rotten, they made faces out of them and sold them to the public under the false pretense that they resembled a famous celebrity.

"You and him, you're together?" he said.

I nodded.

"Huh," he said.

I got the impression he didn't hold Nick in the highest regard, and I wondered why, but before I could say anything more, Nick had parked and got out of the car and walked up the drive. The two men glanced at one another and Nick made it a point to glare at the two plates in my hand, but neither man smiled. No pleasantries were exchanged. Nick blew past Taye Diggs and waltzed into the house like he needed to prove his status in the pecking order. I turned to follow him inside.

"Hey," Taye Diggs said when I started through the

door, "thanks for the food."

I smiled and nodded.

When I shut the door behind me, Nick had settled in on a stool at my bar.

"I came to take you to lunch," he said, "but I can see you've already eaten."

"I got a late start today. If you would have called, I wouldn't have—"

"Yeah, well, happy birthday," he said.

The tone in his voice reminded me of when I went to dinner at some stranger's house with my parents when I was a kid and my mom forced me to go up to the unknown mystery person and thank them for the invite to a house I never wanted to enter in the first place. It was every child's worst nightmare—the strained powwow with the unknown adult.

"I take it you're still upset," I said.

"Still upset? I can't believe the mess you've gotten yourself into."

Even on my birthday he couldn't miss the chance to tell me yet again about what a mistake he thought I'd made. This summed up our life together over the past several months. If he didn't like something, I was sure to hear about it. He missed the reality of how it affected me, and I didn't have the patience for it anymore.

"I need to jump in the shower," I said. "I have a lot to do before the party tonight."

"I'm trying to talk to you, Sloane. Don't you care about what I have to say?"

"If you want to rehash the same topic again, I've said everything I want to say on the subject," I said. "I can't take back what happened, and even if I could, I wouldn't. I know that's not what you want to hear, but I can't help that."

I grabbed a towel out of the hall closet and walked into the bathroom.

"So, what? Discussion over because that's all you have to say?" he said.

I turned away from him and closed my eyes, taking a moment to relax my accelerated heartbeat.

"Let me have this one day, Nick—okay?" I said. "Just this one."

He shook his head.

"I'll see you tonight." he said. He yanked open the front door and hurled it shut behind him. A picture that clung to the wall in my foyer of Gabby and me when we were kids plunged to the floor, and glass eradicated into tiny fragments.

CHAPTER 10

Every year since Gabby died, I always visited her grave on my birthday. I usually went alone, but under the circumstances, flying solo was out of the question. Taye did his best to give me the privacy I needed and kept a comfortable but close distance. The warmth that radiated down from Park City's summer sun filled every inch of me with peace, and being there with Gabby was one of the only places I could go where I felt that way.

"I wish you were still here, Gabby," I whispered, when I reached her headstone. "There are so many things I want to tell you about my life. I feel like I'm just going through the motions while the world spins all around me. You don't know how much I could use your advice right now."

Wherever Gabby was, I was sure she had a flabbergasted look on her face. I had always been the strong one of the two of us. I never leaned on anyone for anything. My life's motto was easily summed up with the familiar words: if it has to be, it has to be me. It's not that I wanted it that way; it was just the way it had always been.

I knelt down and placed the wildflowers in my hands in front of the marble stone, and when I stood back up, I caught a glimmer of something under a rock the size of my fist that sat on top of the center of her headstone. I must have been too swept away in the moment when I first arrived to notice it. I lifted the stone from where it rested. Beneath it was a slip of paper, and it was pink. I set the rock aside and stared at the paper like I was in some kind of trance, but before I had the chance to unfold it, Taye Diggs was at my side. He didn't miss a beat.

"You want me to open it?" he said.

I shook my head.

"I can do it," I said. And I reached out and unfolded it.

YOU'RE COLD, SLOANE MONROE
VERY, VERY COLD

*****

Fifteen minutes later a half a dozen people milled around the gravesite, including Coop. The note and the rock had been preserved in plastic and passed off to the appropriate person, and I doubted I'd ever see it again. I gazed on my sister's grave and couldn't help but focus on all the people who swarmed around it without much care for the young woman whose remains were beneath. It was dusted and searched for prints and evidence that would never be found.

Coop turned to me with a baffled look on his face.

"Since he reached out to me, it might help if we work together on this."

"That your idea of a joke?" Coop said. "Because it's not funny. What makes you think I'd ever work with you?"

I guess the fact the killer had now decided to communicate with me wasn't a good enough reason for him.

"Have you considered for a moment that I might be able to help you?" I said. "I know everything about this case."

Coop sneered and had a look on his face like I'd just asked him to sit with me through every single scene of *The Notebook.*

"Go ahead and laugh," I said. "We'll see who finds him first."

CHAPTER 11

By the time I arrived at Moll's Tavern for dinner, everyone was there, even Nick. With all that was going on between the two of us, I wasn't sure he'd show. And he was there all right, but not with bells on. He appeared to be the only one at the table who hadn't opted to participate in the jovial repartee that was in full swing, which meant he was still pouting over the recent events that rocked our lives.

Maddie's eyes were focused on the chief, who was clearly in awe of her. It was something I didn't see from him too often. Next to them sat Marty, the former mayor of Park City and his wife, and on the other side were some of my old friends from my college days and Gabby's former boyfriend. All in all, it had been a crappy birthday thus far, but my heart swelled to see everyone gathered around the table in spite of all that was going on.

"There's the birthday girl," Maddie shouted when I

walked in.

Everyone at the table gazed up at me at the same time with smiles smeared across their faces—except Nick. He ogled the drink in his hand with all the fascination of a paleontologist who had just discovered a rare dinosaur fossil within the cavity of a rock.

I said my hello's and then walked around the table and sat down next to him.

"I went ahead and ordered your favorite martini," Maddie said.

"Thanks, it's been a long day."

Nick rose from the table, and for a moment, I thought he was going to propose a toast.

"Excuse me for a minute," he said and walked away from the table.

Once he was out of earshot, Maddie piped up.

"What's his freakin' deal?"

"Who knows?" I said.

"Well, don't let his pissy attitude ruin your special night. Besides," she said with a finger pointed to the center of the table, "look at all those presents."

"You guys didn't need to get me anything," I said. "Just being here is enough."

"Oh please, Sloane," Maddie said. "What's a birthday party without presents? I don't care how old I get; it's still all about the gifts. And on that note, I want everyone here to know that my birthday is coming up next month, and early gifts are accepted."

I looked around the table and realized how good it felt to be among friends. Every single person seated there had been an important part of my life in some way. Even the chief, who at the moment was beguiled by Maddie's charms. They'd known each other for years, and never once had I considered them a match.

"How's the birthday girl?" said a voice from behind.

I turned around and almost missed the pint-sized Moll standing beside me. She was the owner of the place. Her fiery-red hair was pulled back into a tight bun that exposed a starry sky of freckles on her circular face.

"Hungry," I said.

She scanned the table.

"What are we having then?"

In unison, everyone spouted off their orders.

"Now hold on right there," Moll said. She took her pen from the top of her ear and angled it in my direction. "One at a time now. Sloane, let's start with you."

I gave my order and then we went down the line, this time in an organized manner.

"And Detective Calhoun," Moll said, "I could have sworn he was here a minute ago, unless my eyesight's gone off the reservation again. Where'd that boy run off to?"

Right here," Nick said.

Moll looked over at him and then placed one hand

on the side of her mouth and leaned toward him. In a whisper she said, "You're flying low tonight, detective."

Nick didn't comprehend her statement, and Moll wasn't the type to wait around until he did. She tried again, this time more plainspoken than before.

"Your zipper, dear, it's undone."

He glanced down and turned away from the table to fix himself up and then sat in his chair and did his best to pretend it never happened.

"I'll get your orders right out," Moll said. "And Sloane, yours is on me tonight."

She walked away and Nick looked at me and smiled for the first time that evening. It seemed forced, but at least it wasn't a scowl.

"What do you say we open your presents while we wait?" Maddie said.

Before I could respond, she'd already dug her hands into the pile and moved them down one by one.

"Mine first," she said.

Maddie's gift was an envelope that contained two gift cards: one to Nordstrom and another for a spa day, and at the moment, I was in desperate need.

"I love this," I said.

"So do I," she said, "it's for two, and by that I mean the two of us are going to have a great time together."

I opened a few more gifts, and then it was time for Nick's. His present was in the smallest package, but the box was an unmistakable bluish color and one every woman on the planet recognized and dreamed of their entire life. Everyone except me, and I tried not to squint when I opened it. Inside was the most beautiful necklace I'd ever laid eyes on, a simple but elegant round pendant with the initial S engraved on the front. I suppressed the urge to breathe a sigh of relief and turned to Nick and smiled.

Nick rose from his chair and separated the necklace from the box and wrapped the dainty piece of silver around my neck.

"Do you like it?" he said.

"It's perfect, thank you."

"One more present to go," Maddie said.

She lifted up the last box and shook it.

"All right," she said, "who got Sloane a gallon of milk for her birthday?"

The last box was wrapped in burgundy paper with felt embossed black lotus flowers all over it. All four sides were adorned with thick, black satin ribbon that rose up the sides and formed a perfect series of bows in the center at the top.

"Wow, you're not kidding," I said to Maddie when I relieved it from her grip. "This thing's heavy. Who's it from?"

I looked around the table and no one uttered a word, and there was no card of any kind affixed to it.

"Oh come on, you guys, who's going to take credit for the best wrap job of the night?"

"Maybe it's a surprise," Maddie said. "And you're not supposed to know who it's from until you open it."

I shook the box in my hands.

"Feels like a bag of flour."

"Come on, Sloane," Maddie said. "Enough with the suspense. Open it already!"

I pulled off the ribbon and took my time removing the paper. I didn't know why; it wasn't like I'd ever use it again, but it was so unique, I didn't want to take the chance of it getting ruined. Once the paper was off, it unmasked a simple white box made of cardboard. I pulled open the lid and peered inside.

"Well?" Maddie said. "What is it? I'm dying over here."

"I'm not sure," I said. "It looks like a bottle of some kind."

I spread my fingers apart and reached down the crevices of the box until they touched the bottom. Clear liquid sloshed around in the container while it rose to the top. Maddie curled her body over the box and pressed her fingers into the sides so it was unable to move while I lifted it. When it was halfway out, the mayor's wife couldn't take the anticipation any longer. With eyes that sparkled like a child full of wonder on Christmas Day, she leaned over to get a closer look and then clamped her hands over her mouth and let out a scream that echoed through the restaurant. In an instant the loud, boisterous atmosphere evaporated until all that remained was silence.

CHAPTER 12

"What in the hell is that?" Maddie said.

The chief and Nick launched out of their respective chairs and hovered over me like a couple of eagles protecting their nest. By the time I had the bottle all the way out of the box, no less than six pairs of eyeballs were riveted on the liquid substance within the glass and what floated around inside of it: a severed finger.

The chief held his hand out to me and folded his fingers back toward himself.

"Lemme see that," he said.

I handed it over and then tipped the box on its side and peered in again. A slip of pink paper was taped flat to the bottom and on it, a message:

HAPPY BIRTHDAY SLOANE MONROE
I HOPE YOU LIKE IT
YOURS ALWAYS, SINNERMAN

"There's a note," I said.

"Don't touch it," the chief said. He flung his arms to the side like he was an umpire who'd just declared the player that slid into home plate safe. "No one touch a thing."

The chief reached over and confiscated the box from me, and with great care he lowered the jar back into the depths of its cardboard home.

"Madison," the chief said.

"I'm way ahead of you," Maddie said. "We can take this to my lab right now."

She stood up and walked over to me and gave me a hug.

"I'm sorry to leave you like this on your birthday sweetie."

"With all that's happened, this trumps my big day," I said. "Keep me posted on what you find out."

She leaned in until she was a couple inches away from my ear.

"You'll be the first to know," she whispered.

Moll returned with a tray full of entrees and a perplexed look on her face.

"Where in the world is everyone going?" she said.

"I'm sorry," I said, "but it looks like we're going to need these to go."

CHAPTER 13

Nick wore a hole in my living room carpet while he paced from one side of the room to the other, part in a debate with himself and another part using his hands to converse with the air in front of him. I rested on the couch and tried to make the most of my entrée to go.

"This has gotten out of hand," he said, after a few minutes. "That psycho has made it personal, and I don't like it."

The reality was it had been personal for a long time now, and we both knew it. Sinnerman had just upped the ante, and for whatever reason, all bets were on me.

"If they can lift a print and find out who this guy is, it will all have been worth it," I said.

I already knew full well the box and its contents would be clean. Sinnerman was too smart for that. But at the moment, my main goal was to pacify Nick by whatever means necessary.

"How can you sit there and eat right now after what just happened?" He shook his head. "You know what? I think you wanted this."

"That's ridiculous," I said.

"Do you even care that this guy could be watching your every move? Honestly, Sloane. I've had it with all this. I'm done. From now on, you're going to listen to me, starting right now. I want you to promise me you won't have anything else to do with this case."

Inside my head, something snapped. All my life I'd been an overachiever, the organized girl with the OCD who tried her best no matter what. I was no quitter. Grandpa instilled that in me from a young age. The Monroes kept going and never gave up. It was our creed. How could he expect me not to go after the one person who took my sister away from me? While I sat and listened to the endless load of crap that spewed forth from Nick's lips, I couldn't take it any longer. It was like something woke up inside me that had been asleep since the day we moved in together. A light came on and I knew what I needed to do. The time had come to flip the switch on our relationship.

"Enough! For the last several months I've had to sit here and listen to you tell me what to do and what not to, and I can't take it anymore!" I said.

My sudden outburst left him unsure of what to say.

"I need some time to myself," I said.

"Fine, I'll sleep on the couch for a while. I did it last night; I don't see why I can't do it again."

I shook my head.

"I need you to leave," I said. "Now."

"Are you kidding me—you're kicking me out?"

"It's not like you don't have a place to go. You haven't sold your place in town yet. You'll be fine. I need this right now."

"You know what; I don't think you mean a word of it. You're not in your right mind because of all that's happened these past few days. You just need some time to get back to yourself again."

"I'm thinking clearer now than I have in a while."

He snatched one of my empty glass canisters from the kitchen counter and heaved it across the room. It smashed against the window, and the glass shattered. In an instant Taye Diggs was through the front door and by my side.

"What's going on here?" Taye said.

"Nothing that concerns you," Nick said. "Get out."

Taye looked at me.

"You okay?"

"She's fine," Nick said. "You can go."

"After you," Taye said, his arm extended toward the door.

"You hard of hearing or something? I told you to go," Nick said.

Taye didn't budge, and neither did Nick. It was like a bar scene from an old Western, but without the pistols.

"Please leave," I said.

"You heard the lady," Nick said. "Get out."

I looked at Nick.

"I didn't mean him, I meant you," I said.

Nick gave me a look that sent a shockwave of chills through my body. It was a side of him I'd never seen before; it felt ice cold, and I didn't like it.

"Unbelievable," Nick said. "I'm here trying to protect you from a complete whack job who's tracking your every move, and this is what I get for it?"

"It's not about that," I said.

"Oh really, what then?"

"It's all of it," I said. "Things haven't been good between us for a while now. I don't know how you can't see it too."

He threw both hands out to the side.

"Fine, if that's what you want, I'm out of here." He turned to Taye Diggs and said, "Have fun with her. She's more than you bargained for, but at least I don't have to deal with it anymore."

"Have some respect, Calhoun," Taye said.

Nick stuck his middle finger out at Taye and then walked into the bedroom and returned a few minutes later with an armful of clothes in his hands. He headed straight for the door and never looked back.

My cell phone rang. It was Maddie.

"Hey," she said, "how are you doing?"

"I just kicked Nick to the curb," I said.

"For good?"

"I don't know yet. What did you find out about the finger?" I said.

"For starters, although I thought so at first, it didn't belong to the woman who was killed the other day."

"Well then, whose is it?" I said.

"Sloane, I don't know how to tell you this."

Suddenly I realized who the finger belonged to, and my food wasn't settled in my stomach anymore. My memory flashed to the nail from the finger that floated around in the jar at the restaurant. It had been coated with a shade of hot pink nail polish that sparkled with flecks of silver glitter. I'd seen it before many times. I squeezed both hands over my mouth, but it didn't matter. I knew I'd never make it to the bathroom in time.

CHAPTER 14

Sam Reids sat at a desk in front of a computer on his newly acquired seventeenth-century George II armchair. It was an expensive piece, and he'd shelled out almost a million dollars for it, but from the moment he'd laid eyes on it when it went up on the auction block, he knew he needed to have it in his collection.

Sam gazed at the picture of Sloane Monroe plastered across the entire width of his computer monitor. It wasn't long before he started to reminisce about the day he first saw her. He'd been on his way to the store to procure a few groceries. When he stopped at the traffic light, he happened to glance over, and there she was. It was like she'd risen from the dead, and he had to do a double-take to make sure his eyes hadn't played some kind of cruel trick on him. It couldn't have been her, and he knew that. He'd killed her over a year before. *But if it isn't Gabrielle Monroe, who is she*, he'd thought. Sam had an insatiable desire to find out, so when he returned home he searched the Internet, and it didn't take long for him to find some answers. Gabrielle Monroe had a sister, and not just any sister—a twin named Sloane. It was all too delicious to take in, and he fantasized over what it would be like to be one of the only serial killers in history to murder twins. Killing Sloane would be like murdering Gabrielle all over again. Just the thought of it caused the hair on his body to stand on end.

Sam had kept a close eye on Sloane over the past two years, and he'd come to know her habits. He knew she visited her sister's grave on special occasions, her favorite place to eat, and even which color she wore the most. Keeping tabs on her while she worked intoxicated him. Her ability to snare the bad guy or find a missing person was impressive, and he admitted to himself after a time that she'd become somewhat of an obsession to him. No woman had ever incited the feelings she did. His insides burned like hot oil simmering in a pan every time he thought of her, and that's why he needed her. He wanted her more than anything he'd ever craved before, but he'd have to wait for now. Sloane was special, which was why he would save her for last, and then everything would be different.

The clock on the right side of Sam's computer displayed 7:29 pm. It was almost time. He closed his eyes and locked his fingers together behind his head, reclining back in his chair. He imagined the rest of the night's events and played them over and over in his head with an exact notion of how they would be. He was the conductor of a fine orchestra. *Let's let the show go on.*

*****

Twenty minutes later Sam trolled the area by the supermarket where he'd discarded his last victim. He snickered when he drove past the parking lot and observed a couple police officers dressed in plain clothes trying to blend in with the pedestrians flowing in and out of the store. *They're all so stupid,* he thought. He never killed in the same location twice. He knew it, and so did they. And yet there they were, grasping at straws like puppets on a string.

Sam drove further down the street and through the city until he reached his destination, the local park. It was uncharted territory, and he'd never abducted anyone in a place like this before, but he'd been there several times over the past few months and was confident in his decision.

The park was quiet, just like he knew it would be. For whatever reason, Thursdays were always like this. There were no games going on, few kids, and the entire place was vacant, save a few stragglers dotting the grass-filled landscape.

Sam laced up his tennis shoes and stepped out his car

door, closing it behind him. He walked over to the dirt track that surrounded the perimeter of the park and set off into a sprint. He rounded the corners, looked around, and sized up the selection. The woman who jogged ten feet in front of him had potential. He amplified his speed until they were side by side and then struck up a conversation, but it didn't take long for him to notice something off about the way her long, dark hair moved when she ran. It didn't. It was thick like it had been coated with the firmest brand of hairspray and then ironed down in place, but that wasn't all; it was fake—a wig, and beneath it he saw patches of dirty blond that looked like it hadn't seen the inside of a hair salon in years. Upon closer inspection, he clued in on something else: her stiff breasts were fake too, and he wondered how much work she'd done on the rest of her body. This repelled him like he was a mosquito and she was doused in bug spray, and he knew she wouldn't do. She wouldn't do at all.

It didn't take long for Sam to notice someone else who would. A woman, with the looks of a young girl still in college, sat alone on a bench with a book in her hand and headphones in her ears. She read in silence, unaware of the element of danger around her. Sam took refuge under a majestic oak tree, waiting for the sun to fade. After a time it lowered itself behind the mountain, producing a glare on the woman like a spotlight which lit her up like the soft glow that protruded from a lighthouse. Sam's heart skipped a couple beats. She was the one.

Thirty minutes went by, but the park was still occupied by four visitors. With every moment that ticked by, Sam's appetite to claim his prize grew more insatiable; but he knew if he persisted, in time his patience would pay off. And ten minutes later it did. There were only two people left in the park now: Sam and the gorgeous brunette on the bench. And soon there would be none.

CHAPTER 15

The next day I sat at the desk at my office. My eyes bored into the business card I held in my hand. It didn't contain a name or an address or the title of a business even. In fact, there was only one thing on it: a phone number. The card had been given to me several months back by a man named Giovanni Luciana. I'd helped his sister out of a bad situation, and he'd tracked me down and offered me his card in case I ever needed him for anything—like some sort of *you-helped-me-so-now-I-need-to-return-the-favor* kind of thing, but I knew nothing about the man except how I felt when we first met. Something about him was unique; he was different than other men I'd been around in the past, and in the brief moments we spent together when we met the first time, he had a big impact on me; there was a certain magnetism that pulled us together. My emotions at the time of our quick rendezvous had been a mix of nervousness and some kind of strange attraction. Or maybe I was beguiled by him, but I didn't know why. Whatever it was, part of me wanted to run that day and get far away from him, but another side of me was curious and hoped I'd find a reason to see him again one day.

I dialed the number listed on the center of the card into my cell phone and waited. It rang once and then a second time, and then my office door opened, and Maddie sauntered in. She plopped down on the chair across from mine and gawked at me.

"So why'd you call me down here then?" she said.

I hit the end call button on the phone and met her gaze. Maybe it was a sign, and I didn't need his help after all.

"I'll tell you in a minute," I said, "but first I want to know more about the finger."

"Well, he did a good job of preserving it. The liquid in the jar he gave you was ethyl alcohol. The tissue in the finger hadn't disintegrated much at all over time, and it was intact enough that we were able to run some tests."

"And you're sure it was Gabby's?" I said.

She nodded.

"There's no doubt about it Sloane—I'm sorry," she said.

"Don't be. He's just trying to unnerve me."

"Yeah well, whoever he is, he's twisted," she said.

"I'll be fine. Besides, I have Taye Diggs, and I'm sure

he won't let anything happen to me."

Maddie crossed her arms and leaned back. "If you say so," she said. "But I know how you work. You take risks, and this might be one of those times you might want to consider your safety for a change."

"So listen," I said, "you know I'd do anything to catch this guy, right?"

"I don't think there's a person around here that isn't aware of that fact," she said.

"I want to show you something, but it's in the vault."

There was a twinkle in her eye, like I'd just given her the keys to the Magic Kingdom.

"Sweet!" she said. "Are we talking covert operations here? If so, I'm in."

"We're talking *I-don't-want-the-chief-to-know-anything-about-it* here."

"Even better. Now I *have* to know," she said.

"And you won't say anything to anyone, right?"

"Sloane," she said. "Wouldn't you agree we're past that point in our relationship? I mean, men are fabulous to have around, and they have their moments, I'm sure most women would agree. But to have a girlfriend who has your back no matter what—no guy is worth that."

I stood up and walked over to a watercolor painting that hung on my wall. It was large, about the size of a sixty-inch, flat-screen TV, the perfect decoy.

"You called me here to discuss a painting?" she said.

"Let me guess, the artist placed something in the background, a hidden clue of some kind, like those weirded-out pictures people used to hang in their bathrooms or in the foyer, and you can't decipher what it is, so you called me here to figure it out for you."

We both laughed.

I shifted my body weight to the right and looked around the corner at Taye Diggs. He manned his post outside, oblivious to the girl talk, which was just how I wanted it to be. When I was sure his eyes were focused in a different direction, I lifted the painting from its position on the wall.

"Holy crap!" Maddie said.

I smiled.

"I don't think obsession is the right word to describe what I'm seeing here," she said.

Behind the painting on the wall was an oversized peg board, and on it was every piece of information I'd come across that related to the Sinnerman murders. There were photos of his female victims, newspaper clippings I'd saved, his killing timeline, a profile I'd created on him, and anything else I felt was relevant to the case.

Maddie sprung from her chair to get a closer look.

"How long have you had this here?" she said.

"I started to piece it together bit by bit a few months after Gabby died."

"This is, like—amazing," she said. "I bet you have

more information here than anyone else on this case."

"I wouldn't go that far," I said. "I haven't been able to get my hands on most of the evidence, not even to copy it, but I did the best I could with what I had access to."

"I'll say," she said. "Nick know about this?"

I shook my head.

"No one does," I said.

Maddie zeroed in on a white piece of lined paper I'd tacked to the wall with the killer's criminal profile on it.

"May I?" she said.

"Go right ahead. It isn't the same one the cops have though—I came up with it on my own."

She lifted the page from the board and read it out loud.

SINNERMAN PROFILE

MALE, AGE 35-45

METHODICAL AND ORGANIZED

SOCIOPATH

KILLS FOR POWER, POSSESSION???

ABUSED   OR   POSSIBLY   NEGLECTED   OR
ABANDONED BY A PARENT

INTELLIGENT, HIGH IQ

CHOOSES WOMEN OF SAME APPROXIMATE AGE,
WEIGHT, HAIR COLOR

Maddie stopped about a quarter of the way through the list and said, "You forgot to add sick lunatic whacko."

"If it's all accurate."

"Oh come on, we both know you have a gift for this kind of thing. I'd be willing to bet you're about ninety-five percent on target with all this."

"The reason I wanted you to see this is because this time I want to be kept in the loop. With his last series of killings I couldn't deal with it, and you and everyone else kept mum."

"We were just trying to help you get through your loss," she said, "and giving you all the details back then wouldn't have been the right thing to do. We all knew that."

"And I agree, but this isn't some kind of blood pact you made with each other where you're obligated to a vow of silence—things are different now. I know you have access to a lot of information, and I want you to share it with me."

I stared her right in the eye and tried to gauge her reaction. She cocked her head to one side like she had taken it all in and then said, "Fine by me."

"I bet the chief is going to tell you things too since the two of you are together now. You are still an item, right?"

"Item is taking it a bit far," she said. "You know how I roll. I just go with it, I never define it."

Maddie didn't like to get too committed to her men.

It made her feel like she did when she was in high school and her mother strapped her down at home with all her siblings and she missed out on all the things most teens experience at that time of their life. Her preferred method of dating only worked if it was done on her own terms, which was why it surprised me that she agreed to date the chief in the first place.

"Don't worry," she said. "I'll tell you as much as I can. But I want you to do something for me in return."

"Anything."

"Be careful," she said.

"Always."

"I mean it, Sloane. I worry about you," she said.

Maddie's cell phone rang.

"How's it going, babe?" she said into the receiver.

"You're calling him *babe* now?" I whispered loud enough for only her to hear. "When did that happen?"

She grinned and shushed me with her finger, but within a few seconds, the look of glee on her face turned to genuine concern, and she ended the call without another word.

"What is it?"

"Sinnerman's killed again," she said.

I grabbed my keys from the top of my desk. "I'll drive."

CHAPTER 16

The body had been disposed of in the center of the track at the city park. I was thankful when I looked around and noted that Nick and Coop weren't there yet. A mass of spectators had gathered behind the thin, plastic, roped-off section of police tape.

Maddie stepped inside the perimeter and flashed her credentials to a male officer I didn't recognize. As the head ME for various counties, she always got in easily. The same couldn't be said for me.

"And who's this?" he said and thumbed in my direction.

"She's with me," Maddie said.

He shifted his attention from her to me.

"Where's your ID, lady?" he said.

"Look," Maddie interjected, "we just came from lunch, and it's not like I had the time to swing by my office so she could grab it. It seemed more important to me at the time to get here as soon as possible, so why don't you lay off and let us do our job."

He didn't seem to know what to say, so he let us pass. It didn't buy me a lot of time, but it bought me a little, and I was determined to make every second count. I glanced back at Taye Diggs who shook his head but didn't try to stop me.

Maddie approached a young male who was hunched over the dead woman's body collecting various tidbits of evidence.

"What do you got for me?" she said.

"From what I can tell, the victim appears to have been killed less than twenty-four hours ago, and it looks like her wounds are an identical match to the woman killed the other day. Everything matches up except the number of lacerations to her thigh."

I leaned in and counted them. There were five this time.

"Do we have a name?" Maddie said.

"She had an ID card from a university not far from here in her back pocket. Her name is Sasha Winters."

"She looks a little old to be a university student."

A car drove up and parked and out stepped public enemy number one and two.

"Uh-oh," Maddie said. "Get ready for an ass-chewing sandwich."

I retrieved my cell phone from my pocket with haste

and snapped some photos of the victim and the crime scene and then slid it back into my pocket.

"Why is it that wherever I go, you seem to follow?" Coop said.

"I was with Maddie when she got the call."

"And that makes it all right?" he said.

"It makes it the truth."

"Here's some truth for you—I want you out of here. Now."

I looked over at Nick whose crossed arms told me all I needed to know about where he stood in all of it, and then I turned toward Maddie.

"I'll catch a ride back to my lab with one of my guys," she said. "You go on."

"Call me later?" I said.

She smiled and nodded. Everyone else frowned.

CHAPTER 17

The next morning I reappeared at the crime scene, but the difference was the body wasn't there and everything had been cleaned up and life at the park was back to usual. It was hard to tell anything had happened there at all. I wasn't sure what I was looking for or why anything of any significance would have been left behind, but I wanted to explore the area anyway. It was of particular interest to me that the killer dropped his bodies off in the same place he picked them up. He was bold, and had one mad pair of cojones. That much I knew.

Maddie had called me the night before with some privileged information she'd been given about the victim. The girl had gone to the park the night before to study, like she often did during the week. Her mother told the police there was a specific bench she liked to sit on so they dusted it for prints, but I knew Sinnerman's wouldn't be among them. I sat on the bench, scanned the area, wondering if he watched her and for how long. I envisioned him hunkered down somewhere while he watched and waited, and I searched around to see if I could find the most likely spot. Some nine or so yards away, the leaves on a lofty oak tree sprawled out in all directions across a pale-blue sky. It was the only one of its kind in the immediate area, and the bushes surrounding it offered the perfect place for a person to hide.

I approached the tree and crouched down and scanned the ground that surrounded me. There were no footprints, but there was a patch of dirt that appeared to have been smoothed over by something, like it didn't belong with the sediment around it. In my stooped position, I had a clear view of the bench. I stayed there for a few minutes and absorbed the scene and then withdrew my phone from my pocket and took a picture of it. I didn't know why; it just seemed like it was the right thing to do. I tilted the lens downward and zoomed in and snapped a photo of the disheveled patch of the dirt. The more I looked at it, the more I noticed something odd. The dirt around it was undisturbed and looked like it had been for quite some time.

I brushed the rough patch of dirt back and forth with my hand. It was loose, and in no time, I'd dug a good three inches at least. I extracted the mound of dirt into my hand and stared down into the miniature hole I'd formed. I felt like a kid in grade school who had nothing better to do to pass the time at recess. I tilted my hand to the side and watched the dirt tumble back into the hole, and with it, a little piece of debris about the size of a nickel dropped into the hole as well. It was dirty and crumpled and had been folded at least five times to get it to its current size. I scooped it out of the hole and opened it.

> I ALWAYS KNEW YOU WERE BETTER THAN THEM.
>
> THAT IS WHAT I LIKE ABOUT YOU.
>
> YOU DON'T THINK LIKE A COP.
>
> YOURS ALWAYS, SINNERMAN
>
> P.S. YOU'RE GETTING WARMER.

Did he mean them—the guys on the case, or them—the women. Or both?

"Excuse me," a voice said, "are you a cop?"

I stood up and came face to face with a woman dressed in a pair of fluorescent yellow shorts and a tank top that was cut so low I caught more than a glimpse of what a little breast enhancement can do for a person. On her eyes she donned a pair of hot-pink sunglasses, which hid a fraction of her face from me.

"Something like that," I said.

"I feel just awful about what happened to that poor young woman yesterday," she said.

And yet, here she was parading herself around like a

nosy tourist.

Taye Diggs approached from the right. I tried to indicate I didn't need him, but he charged forward anyway. I made a fist with my right hand and concealed the note I'd found within my palm. This one was mine.

I looked at the woman.

"Is there something I can do for you?" I said.

"Actually, there is," she said. "After I got home last night, I got to thinking about everything, and I thought I might be able to help."

"How?" I said.

"I might be able to give you a description."

I looked at Taye and tried to restrain the urge I felt to give him a high five. We both stared back at her, speechless.

"Were you at the park last night?" I said.

She nodded.

"Around what time?"

"Oh, I got here about a quarter to eight, went around the track a couple times and then went home. You see, I don't usually come out to the park. I like to get my workouts in at home, but a couple days ago my treadmill broke. I bought another one, but my husband has been too busy to set it up for me, and I'm too small to lift it."

I wondered how long she would go on with her personal life story if I didn't stop her.

"Did you see anyone or anything suspicious while

you were here?" I said.

She nodded again.

"I saw a strange man."

"Where?" I said.

"When I was running."

"On the track?" I said.

"That's right. He ran beside me for a minute."

This was the first time in Sinnerman's history that there was an actual sighting—if it turned out to be true. Could he have slipped up?

"He talked to you?" I said.

"Not in so many words," she said. "But he did say hello and mentioned something about the weather we were having that day and how summer was his favorite season of the year. He was going on and on about the arts festival—you know the one where people display their paintings on Main Street?"

"Yeah—that was a couple months ago. Anything else?"

"When he finished, I looked over to respond, and he frowned at me and took off."

It wasn't hard for me to see why. She wasn't his type. From behind, he may not have known it, but once he got close, he wouldn't have chosen her. I was sure of it.

I reached for the card-sized notepad in my back pocket and a pen.

"What did he look like?" I said.

"That's what I thought was strange. Here this guy was gushing about how warm it was at the festival, and he was wearing a charcoal hoodie. It didn't make sense to me. I mean, it must have been eighty degrees at the time of day, and he was jogging no less."

Her eyes shifted from me to a bird that flew by in front of us. I needed to speed things up.

"How tall would you say he was?" I said.

"Well," she said, "he was taller than me for sure. Not by much though. He only had about three inches on me."

"So around five ten?"

"That'd be about right."

"What about hair color, eye color?" I said.

"He wore dark glasses that made him look like a beetle, and I don't mean the car. And his hair was perfect."

"How so?" I said.

"Well, he had that hoodie on so it was hard to tell for sure, but at one point while he was talking to me he lifted it a bit and stuck his hand inside and smoothed it out, like a piece had strayed and it bugged him. From what I could see, it was a brownish color, and he had it parted to one side—I'd say twenty-five percent to the left and the rest to the right."

"Was it thick, thin, receding?" I said.

"Thick."

"Long or short?"

"Short."

"Eyes?" I said.

"He never took the glasses off."

"Do you know where he went after you talked to him?"

She shook her head.

"I didn't pay him any attention after he gave me the brush off. I left."

Taye Diggs took out his cell phone and dialed.

"I'm going to need you to do something for me," I said to the woman.

"All right."

"Head down to the police station. They'll take your official statement," I said. "And I'm sure they'll want to get a sketch of the guy while it's still fresh in your mind."

I took her name, address, and phone number down and then sent her on her way. What a day it had been already, and it was just getting started.

CHAPTER 18

When I arrived back to my car, a silver Aston Martin idled behind it, which blocked me from backing out. The window tint was so dark on the driver's side, I couldn't have seen in even if I had a flashlight. Taye Diggs opened my car door and took his hand, shoved me inside, and drew his gun.

"Get down," he said, "until I find out who this is."

I squatted low enough in the seat that I was well below the window but still high enough to watch all the action through the side mirror. The window of the Aston Martin came down and unveiled a face I hadn't seen in months, and I gasped loud enough for everyone on the street to hear.

I opened the door of the car.

"I told you to stay inside," Taye said through clenched teeth.

I looked toward the other car.

"Giovanni?" I said. "What are you doing here? How did you find—"

"It's nice to see you again Sloane," Giovanni said.

Taye looked over at me and then at Giovanni.

"Are you gonna tell me who this dude is or what?" Taye said.

Giovanni stuck out his hand to Taye. "The name is Giovanni Luciana," he said, "can I speak with you for a moment?"

Taye looked at me.

"It's all right," I said. "We know each other. You can put your gun down."

The truth was I didn't know him. Not well, anyway.

Taye made the most of his muscular frame and held his arms at his side the way an ape did while he walked over to Giovanni's car. Once there they engaged in small talk that wasn't audible enough for me to hear. From the look on his face, Taye wasn't happy. He made a phone call and frowned and then looked at Giovanni like he wanted to inflict blunt-force trauma to various parts of his body.

"She's all yours," Taye said to Giovanni.

What was that supposed to mean?

Giovanni stepped out of the car and walked over to the passenger side door and opened it and gestured inside with his hand.

"Come with me please," he said to me.

"What—why?"

"You'll see," he said.

"It's fine," Taye said. "He'll explain everything, just go with him."

I was both reluctant and exhilarated, which up until then, I didn't know could be experienced at the same time. I walked over to the car and got in and looked at Taye who nodded at Giovanni and then turned and went.

What was happening?

"Do you want to tell me what's going on?" I said to Giovanni.

"We're going for a drive," he said.

"May I ask where?"

"You'll see."

Why was it that everything surrounding him was always shrouded in secrecy? I was unnerved, but not enough that I didn't absorb everything about him—the way he was dressed in an expensive charcoal suit with light-grey pinstripes, the Montblanc watch on his wrist—even his mannerisms and the way he flicked his wrist when he shifted gears with his long, bony fingers had an element of fascination to it.

"Why did you hang up on me yesterday?" he said.

"How did you know I'd be here today?"

"You first," he said.

"All right. Someone came in after I dialed your number, and I decided I didn't know why I called in the first place, so I hung up."

He held his pointer finger up in the air.

"Ah, but you do know, don't you? Something compelled you to call me," he said. "I can hear it in your voice now as you talk to me. What was it?"

From the sound of it, I wasn't going to get away with evading his questions for long, but there wasn't a level of comfort required for me to open up and spill it all out either. The shield to my circle of trust was up, and he was on the outside.

"I was thinking about the first time we met several months ago," I said.

"I remember it well," he said. "You accused me of murdering that poor excuse for a man who used my sister's body as part of his daily workout routine."

"And I still think so."

That did it. In a moment of haste, I'd spoken about the suspicions I had about him over the past several months. The words gushed out of my mouth too fast for me to do anything, like they often did, and now they clung in the air between us like a leaf desperate to stay welded to the branch of a tree.

His eyebrow lifted.

"I shouldn't have—"

"You say what's on your mind, and I respect that," he said. "It's an admirable quality."

"When I asked about your involvement, you didn't

deny it."

"I never admitted it either," he said. "Wouldn't you agree the women of the world are better off without him? Who knows how many more women he would have abused?"

We both sat for a minute, and neither of us said a word. We just drove. Destination: unknown.

After a few minutes of silence, he said, "Where does that leave us?"

I shook my head.

"I don't even know you."

"Don't you?" he said.

What is that supposed to mean?

"You checked into my background right after we first met," he said. "I would say you know quite a bit."

The man didn't miss a beat. I thought about asking him how he knew, but then we'd be back to going in circles again. It was unusual. For some reason our exchange made me feel like I was the one being interrogated, instead of the other way around, and in that moment, the tables had been turned—on me.

I glanced in the side mirror at the car a short distance behind that had mimicked Giovanni's every move. It had been that way for the past two miles or so.

Giovanni looked over at me and then in his rear view mirror.

"Don't worry about them," he said. "They're with

me."

"They were around the last time we spoke as well. What are they, some sort of protection?"

"In a way, yes," he said.

"Are you always this elusive?"

He laughed.

"Do you always ask so many questions?" he said.

"Yes."

"I have eyes and ears everywhere. I make it a point to know what I need to know when I need to know it."

In a way, he'd answered my question, but in another way, he hadn't answered it at all.

"Talk to me about this case," he said, "about Sinnerman. I want to know all about him."

"I'm not sure why you're interested," I said.

His face looked stern, but he didn't seem dismayed by my comment.

"Let me ask you something—do you believe I can help you?" he said. "Is that why you called me?"

I thought about it for a moment, but it wasn't necessary for me to answer. From the first moment I'd laid eyes on him when we met, I knew he was a force to be reckoned with, a man in some kind of powerful position. My gut instinct gave me a good idea of what that was, but I didn't want to believe it. I took a deep breath in, and when I exhaled, out came the entire back-story of my sister, Sinnerman, the latest slayings of more innocent women—all of it.

When I finished he said, "What is it you would like me to do?"

It was the moment of truth.

"I hoped you could help me nail the son of a bitch."

"And when I do—what then?"

"You're very sure of yourself," I said. "No one got anywhere close to figuring out who this guy was last time. He knows what he's doing."

"So do I, and you didn't answer my question."

Inside my head the question had already been answered, a hundred times over—maybe more. But to say it out loud? I wasn't sure I could do it. My job had always been to bring people to justice, find the bad guy and let the cops do the rest. But this was different—it was personal, and now I didn't just have sympathy for all the families of victims whose lives had been lost for no reason, I had empathy. And empathy wanted a lot more than a lifetime in prison. Empathy wanted revenge.

I'd been so caught up inside myself I hadn't noticed my finger and the incessant tap dance it was doing on the armrest of the car door. Giovanni took notice and placed his hand on my shoulder. It stopped me right in my tracks.

"Leave everything to me," he said.

"But you don't even know me. Why would you—"

"I learned all I needed to the first time we met.

There's something different about you, Sloane Monroe. You have a drive most people don't possess, and you're selfless. What you did for my sister proved that, and I am in your debt."

"Honestly, you don't owe me anything. I don't view it like that, I never have."

"Then try to see it from a different perspective," he said. "I'm doing this because I want to."

Giovanni turned and parked in front of the police station.

"Why are we——"

He didn't respond. He exited the car and came around to my side and opened the door for me. It felt weird. The last time anyone had grabbed the door for me was on the night of my senior prom, and he only did it because he had one thing in mind at the time, and it wasn't dancing.

Giovanni stretched out his hand to me.

"Come with me," he said. "It's about to get interesting."

CHAPTER 19

All eyes were on the two of us when we walked through the station doors. Nick's in particular. I felt like the main event at the circus, the one the audience waited all night to see. Nick leaned over the side of his cubicle and stared Giovanni down like a lion sizing up his opponent before they battled to determine who would be the one true king. Giovanni didn't seem to notice. Either that or he didn't really care.

The chief was in a glass-enclosed room off to the side with a few other people. He stood when he saw me and opened the door.

"Sloane, in here," he said.

I walked past Nick's desk and couldn't hide the smirk I was sure I had on my face. It felt good to be a part of the "in crowd." I entered the room with Giovanni, and we took a seat. The chief looked at both of us and didn't seem the least bit concerned about who Giovanni was or why he was there.

"Sloane, this is Special Agent Luciana," the chief said with his thumb bent toward a man in a navy suit that I'd never seen before in my life.

If I had a drink I was sure I would have choked on it.

"Did you say Luciana?" I said.

The man stood and exchanged glances with Giovanni. They smiled at one another like they were part of a covert society, and I waited for a secret handshake to take place. When it didn't, he turned his attention to me.

"Special Agent Carlo Luciana. And you must be Miss Monroe."

I took his hand and shook it. It was cold, but firm.

"It's Sloane," I said.

"I hear your grandfather used to be in the FBI."

"He did," I said. "He was a good man."

"You look confused," Agent Luciana said. "Let me explain."

I was, but not just about why he was there.

"Effective immediately, my team is taking over this case," he said. "I have a group of other agents I've brought along to assist me, and we will work together with everyone here until Sinnerman is caught and put away for the rest of his life. I want this to be a team effort with your chief and myself exchanging information. My hope is that the process will run in a cohesive manner."

"I'm a PI," I said. "I don't work for the department, so

I'm not sure why you're telling me all this."

"I understand our serial has been in contact with you—left notes, and that sort of thing."

I nodded.

"Have you heard from him since your birthday party?" he said.

I shook my head. Giovanni slanted his eyes at me but didn't utter a word or change the relaxed expression on his face. Was it possible he knew about the note I'd found earlier that day?

Agent Luciana continued.

"I understand your sister was the last of his first series of victims a few years ago," he said.

"That's right."

"I'm sorry. That must have been hard on you," he said.

"It won't be once he's stopped."

"Trust me when I say that we will do everything we can to do just that."

Agent Luciana looked at the chief.

"I'd like to have a few minutes with Sloane alone," he said.

The chief nodded, and he and Giovanni exited the room.

Once the door closed, I turned toward him.

"You said your last name was Luciana," I said.

"That's right."

"I assume when Giovanni picked me up, that was your doing?" I said.

"I needed to speak with you, yes."

"And the two of you are somehow related?" I said.

"I'm supposed to be the one asking the questions, Miss Monroe."

He sounded just like Giovanni, the way he spoke to me in his calm, collected tone of voice, and in the manner that he constructed his comments. And his eyes, while softer than Giovanni's, had the same dark sheen to them. I was convinced they were connected somehow.

"I have a right to know what's going on here," I said, "and if you want me to answer your—"

"Fair enough," he said. "No need for you to get all worked up. Giovanni is my brother."

I should have been shocked by this, but I wasn't.

"And is he—"

"FBI?"

I nodded. Carlo shook his head and placed his hand over his mouth like he was trying to resist the urge to laugh.

"Why is he here then?" I said.

Carlo smiled and folded his arms and rested them on the table in front of me. He took his time before he replied.

"Let's just say he has a vested interest in this case and leave it at that. Now to my questions for you…."

Meaning me? I couldn't think of any other reason he'd be there. I wanted to continue our back and forth banter until I had more answers, but somehow I already knew I wouldn't get much more out of him, and he looked like he'd said too much already.

"What do you want to know?" I said.

"Everything, but let's start with your sister."

I relayed the information about Gabby, most of which I was sure he had already been briefed on by someone else. When I finished, he nodded and said, "Tell me how you came to be the center of Sinnerman's affections."

This, too, I was sure he knew, but I humored him with what had gone on over the past week since the murders started up again.

"He seems quite taken with you," he said. "How do you feel about that?"

"If it helps us catch him, I'm fine with it."

He moved his hand across the desk and grabbed a file folder, which he placed it in front of him and opened. My name was typed in bold letters in the center across the top. I couldn't read what was below, but it was apparent it was a file about certain moments in my life.

"How long have you been a PI?" he said.

"Is that some kind of profile on me?"

"It's just a little information to help me get to know you better," he said.

"Why?"

"This Sinnerman—the killer, is neat, wouldn't you say?"

I nodded.

"And careful," he said. "To the degree that he's never left behind a print or any type of evidence that would give us any clues to his identity. And then you come into the picture and all of the sudden he takes risks. Why do you think that is?"

"He wrote Coop."

"But the letters to Detective Cooper a few years back weren't like the ones he writes you—these are more personal, intimate."

"There's history between us because of my sister. Look, I think you're wasting your time focusing on these letters."

"What do you suggest?"

"The cops have always centered on the women. They interview their families, look into their background—that's what they did last time, and it's no different now. The women were random. Wrong place, wrong time. It's not like he has any rhyme or reason about who he chooses beyond their age and hair color. Without evidence on Sinnerman, he's been impossible to find so I understand why everyone wants to shift their attention to the women. They're the next best thing. But I believe it will lead to the same place it always has—nowhere."

"What would you suggest?" he said.

I uncrossed my legs, leaned forward in my chair, and looked him right in the eye.

"Forget the women. Focus on Sinnerman, and you'll find him."

"Do you want to know what I think, Miss Monroe?"

I shrugged.

"I think you are the key to whether or not we find him, and that the steps we need to take all begin and end with you," he said.

Before I could respond, the office door opened, and Rose poked her head in.

"Sorry to interrupt," she said, "but the sketch that woman from the park gave us is finished." Rose looked over at Agent Luciana. "I thought you might like to know."

She then turned and closed the door. He stood up and walked toward the door. I remained seated.

"You coming?" he said.

I tried my best not to hide my surprise.

"You want me in there with everyone else?"

"Like I said before, there's a reason our killer is corresponding with you," he said, "and I intend to keep you close while I prove that theory."

"I already have a shadow," I said.

He shook his head.

"Not anymore."

I'd started to grow fond of Taye Diggs. In the short

time I'd known him, I liked having him around. I wasn't ready to see him go—not yet.

"What do you mean by that?" I said.

"I've already assigned some of my men to you."

"More than one? When will I get to meet them?" I said.

"I don't believe that's necessary. If they do what they're supposed to, you won't even know they're around, but rest assured Miss Monroe—they will be. And then of course, you'll also have Giovanni."

"Giovanni—why?" I said. "You said he wasn't FBI so why would he stick around?"

"Gio is the best protection anyone could ask for. You'd be safer with him than ten of my best men. Besides, it's what he wants, and I can't deny my brother's request."

The fog in my head lifted, and I saw a clear picture of what I'd missed before. There was only room for one Alpha male in the Luciana family, and Agent Carlo Luciana wasn't it.

CHAPTER 20

Agent Luciana, the chief, Coop, and I stood in a room and ogled the rendering the sketch artist had come up with. It didn't look much different than a sketch of every other perp in a hoodie that I'd seen. In fact, it was very unibomber-esque.

Agent Luciana looked at me.

"What do you think?" he said.

Coop frowned. He didn't approve of the fact that my opinion was the first one that was solicited. I smiled—wide.

"I'm not sure how much help it will be," I said. "This looks like most of the locals in this town."

He gave the sketch to the chief.

"Get it to the papers," Agent Luciana said. "No matter how average it looks, it sends a message to the killer."

"Which is?" Coop said.

"That he slipped up, and we know about it," Carlo

said. "It may not be much, but it's a start. If we can rile him up, he might make a mistake again."

Through the office window I glanced at Giovanni when I thought he couldn't see me. He was leaning up against the back of a desk with his arms folded. His eyes were centered on something, but I couldn't see what from my vantage point. I leaned over a bit and realized it wasn't a what, it was a who. Nick thrust the door open and aimed all his frustration in my direction.

"What's she doing in here?" he said. "I'm getting really tired of this."

He turned toward the chief who looked at Agent Luciana.

"Can I help you with something?" Agent Luciana said.

"Yeah, you can tell me why Sloane is in this room with you guys and I'm not. She has no business being here."

"That's not for you to decide," Agent Luciana said.

"The hell it isn't," Nick said.

Agent Luciana was unfazed by this. He looked at me, then Coop, then the chief…and without saying a word, we all knew what he wanted. The three of us left the room. Behind closed doors Agent Luciana and Nick went back and forth, voices raised.

Giovanni caught my arm when I walked by.

"Where are you off to?" he said.

"That's a good question. I don't know what I'm supposed to be doing. I feel like I've been assigned a bunch of babysitters."

"I wouldn't look at it like that," he said. "You hungry?"

I nodded. Food did sound good. It had been hours since I'd eaten anything.

"Great," he said. "I know just the place."

Nick stormed out of the office and headed straight for me.

"Who's this guy then?" he said with his thumb pointed in Giovanni's direction. "First you strut in here with him like he's your buddy ol' pal, and now he's taking you to dinner? You don't waste any time."

"Nick, you don't know what you're—"

"You know what? Save it Sloane. It doesn't matter."

Giovanni stepped forward and created a barrier between us.

"I believe you've said enough," Giovanni said.

"I don't know where you get off even talking to me, but if I were you, I'd back off—now."

From across the room Agent Luciana sprang into action until Giovanni held his hand up, and then he halted like he was frozen in time.

Giovanni looked at Nick.

"It would be in your best interest to watch your tone," he said. "And I want you to understand something. This will be the only time I extend that courtesy to you."

Nick sneered and shook his head.

"You know what?" Nick said. "Both of you can go to—"

"Calhoun!" the chief said. "Enough."

Nick hesitated, but it was enough to keep him from foot in mouth disease. He gave me a look that indicated "our" discussion wasn't over, then turned and went.

CHAPTER 21

A half hour later Giovanni and I shared a few rolls at an outside table on Main Street. The sun hadn't set yet, but it had inched its way toward the side of the mountain. I loved this time of day. The sky changed color and produced an array of shades in purple, pink, and blue that I could sit and stare at for hours. It was just one of the aspects I had come to love about life in Park City.

"So where are these guys who are my new keepers?" I said.

"You don't need to worry about that."

I turned to my left and tipped my head toward a man who flew solo at a table not far from us. About every third minute, he fiddled with his wristwatch.

"Is it him?" I said. "Because I've had my eye on him since we got here, and he fits the description."

"Why does it matter?" Giovanni said. "My men are in place so that they can protect you."

His men? So much for his brother leading me to believe I would be chaperoned by the FBI.

"I know how much solving this case means to you," he said. "That's why I'm here."

"I feel like I'm at a table full of men who have mapped out a plan for me, and I'm the only one who's not in on it."

"It was never my intention for you to feel that way," he said, "and if that's the case, I apologize."

"You show up after months, and then your brother turns out to be the head of the FBI team that's over the investigation. A bit too much of a coincidence—even for me—wouldn't you agree?"

"In my line of work I find it's best to have people I can rely on in many different positions. Over time we've learned that this is the best way to…"

To…what? His arms went back to a folded position which told me one thing—he wasn't going to say anything more on the matter.

"This case is everything to me," I said. "And I can't just sit on the sidelines while everyone else runs around and searches for this guy. I just can't."

Giovanni leaned closer to me and reached over and took my hand and enfolded it in his.

"Find him then," he said. "I'm not here to stop you."

I was more confused than the time I was in line at the post office and a woman approached me from behind and said, "Your shirt is on inside out, dear," and I had no idea how it got that way. I couldn't take my eyes off his hand on my hand and how they melded together like ebony and ivory, and I had the sudden urge to pull back, but I didn't.

"I need to do this my way, on my own terms," I said. "I've never been good at, well, working with other people. I can't think unless I'm on my own; it's the way I've always been."

He nodded.

"Whatever you need," he said.

I'd spent the last several months of my life in a debate with Nick where I felt like I needed his permission to take any case that involved the slightest degree of danger, and now here I was with Giovanni, a man I didn't know, who seemed to be interested in one thing—my happiness. It was liberating.

"What do you get out of all this?" I said. "I don't understand why a total stranger like me is even worth your time. Don't you have a lot of other things you're supposed to be doing?"

He averted the question.

"If we are to work together, I do need one thing from you," he said.

"What's that?"

"I want you to tell me everything you know," he said.

"I just spent the afternoon going over all of this at the

station."

"Yes, and now I need you to tell me whatever it is you didn't tell my brother," he said.

"What makes you think I kept anything from him?"

He released my hand and then placed his in front of me palm-side up.

"What is it that you want?" I said.

"I have every confidence that you know."

I was right, he did know about the note I found in the park.

"I guess it won't do me any good to ask how you know about the note," I said.

"I suppose not."

I reached into my pocket and provided him the note. He read it and then folded it back up and gave it back to me.

"This guy thinks he's smart, and he must thrive off the confidence he has in himself. But I have a feeling you're a lot smarter."

*****

An hour later, we were back at the park so I could retrieve my car.

"Thanks for everything," I said. "I appreciate what you are trying to do for me, but I want to give you one last chance to reconsider. I can manage on my own."

He leaned in until he was so close I could feel his

breath on my cheek, and I thought he would kiss me. I wasn't sure what to do or even if I wanted him to or not. I closed my eyes and stuck out my lips just enough to make them seem more inviting, and then I felt his hand flit back and forth on my shoulder. When I opened my eyes he said, "You had a bug crawling up your shirt."

"Oh," I said. "Thanks."

All I could think about was how glad I was that I couldn't see my face in the mirror at that moment.

"I'll say goodnight then," he said. "Until tomorrow."

CHAPTER 22

It was interesting how serene the house had become without Nick there, and I couldn't decide how I felt about it. One thing I did know was that I liked the quiet; I basked in it. And I also liked being alone. There was something to be said for being in charge of your own domain. Now I could watch all those girlie shows without any rebuff from the peanut gallery.

With Nick gone, Lord Berkeley had taken over as man of the house. Steadfast in his newly acquired position, he roosted atop the sofa and performed a scan of the immediate area outside the house. But the stage had long since faded to black, and I wasn't sure his efforts would yield any results.

I entered my bathroom and twisted the knob on my jetted tub. Water spewed forth from the spout and then trickled down and formed a pool. I grabbed some bath salts out of the cabinet and poured them in, and then when I thought I'd sprinkled in a sufficient amount, I peppered in a little more. I couldn't remember the last time I'd used my tub, but I knew one thing; it had been too long.

I lit the candles on the windowsill and settled in to unwind from the long day. So much had happened that was unexpected. Seeing Giovanni again left me with mixed feelings. I knew so little about him, and yet there he was, ready to drop everything in his life and help me. Why? I couldn't believe it was because he felt he owed me some type of favor. There had to be more to it than that.

My thoughts turned to Sinnerman, whoever he was, and about whether we'd be able to stop him before he killed again. I hated to think of it, but my guess was that we would fail, and it was possible it would happen more than once before he was within our grasp. The second victim had been taken five days after the first, and that didn't leave me a lot of time. Two days had already gone by, and I still had little to go on save the paper he'd jotted his terse notes on. The fed's were hard at work on their end, and now it was time for me to do some of my own research.

I stepped out of the tub and followed the sound of my cell phone to my room.

"Hey Maddie," I said.

"How'd everything go today?"

"I don't know—good, I guess."

"Why am I not swayed by that?" she said. "Spit it out."

"I just don't have a handle on things like I want to. I don't even have a clear direction."

"Maybe not yet," she said. "But I know you, and I'm sure you will."

She popped a huge bubble into the phone.

"You never talked to me about the second victim," I said.

"I knew you'd say that. That's why I called. There's not much to tell though."

"You never know," I said. "Sometimes the smallest things make the biggest difference."

"She was a bit younger than some of his other victims by a few years."

"I don't think age has much to do with it. For him, it's more about convenience," I said. "An easy target. What else?"

"This one fought back which would be the first time since…"

She stopped short.

"It's okay," I said. "It would be the first time a woman has fought back since he took Gabby."

"I think he underestimated her—his latest victim. I found definite signs of a struggle. She had a few lacerations on her right hand that were consistent with a six-and-a-half-inch blade, which also seems to be what he uses to slice their legs. But, he cleaned the vic's entire body before he dumped it."

"He's intelligent enough never to leave any evidence behind," I said.

"So that's about it," she said. "Not much to tell. You got any more questions for me?"

"Just one," I said. "What do you know about the mafia?"

CHAPTER 23

Maddie sat across from me and shoveled a spoonful of scrambled eggs in her mouth.

"Thanks for having me over for breakfast," she said.

"I'm glad you came."

She took her fork and turned it to the side and cut her sausage into five pieces and then launched one of the pieces off the side of her plate. It flew through the air like a miniature Olympian doing the catapult and then plopped on my tile floor.

"Maddie," I said, "Boo is spoiled enough as it is."

Lord Berkeley snatched the piece of meat and moved all four paws across the room at rapid speed to the corner where he could enjoy the fruits of his labor in solitude.

"Oh come on, you know I can't resist him when he gives me his pouty eyes."

Few could refuse him when faced with his long, sad stare, and that was the reason he did it.

"Honestly, Sloane, you have the most vivid imagination of anyone I know," she said.

"What are you talking about?"

"Your suspicions last night about Giovanni being in the mafia."

"I'm serious."

"I know you are," she said. "That's why it's so funny."

"You tell me what line of work he's in then," I said. "He drives a car that's worth more than my house, and one of his suits is probably the equivalent of my entire wardrobe."

She tilted her fork toward me.

"Minus your shoe collection, of course," she said.

"You know what I mean."

"And that makes him some mafia person who takes people out for a living?" she said.

"I don't know if he kills anyone," I said. "Maybe his posse takes people out for him."

"I'm pretty sure they don't call it a posse," she said.

Maddie stabbed two spoonfuls of eggs onto her fork and placed them inside her mouth on both sides of her cheeks. She scrunched up four fingers, pressed them into her thumb and held them in the air and transformed herself into a character from *The Godfather*.

"Listen to me Sloane Monroe," she said, "I have this like amazing kind of offer that you—"

"Nice accent, but you're not even close by the way."

"I thought that was pretty damn good," she said.

"Look, the guy is into something; I just can't figure out what."

"So, you've tried?" she said.

"What?"

"To find out who he is?" she said.

I shot her a wink.

"What kind of PI would I be if I didn't?"

"You run a background check while you were at it?" she said.

"Maddie, be serious."

"You did!" she said. "I can tell. You need to chill. From what you've told me about this guy, he'd be much more inclined to whisk you away somewhere for dinner in his private jet than bust a cap in your ass."

"Nice."

She smiled.

"I want to show you something," I said.

"Don't tell me," she said with a wink, "you have a secret peg board here too?"

"Better."

I pulled out the folded piece of paper I uncovered at the park. Maddie raised an eyebrow.

"Is that what I think it is?" she said.

I nodded.

"I can't believe they let you keep that," she said.

I glanced at her but said nothing.

She brought her hand to her mouth.

"Sloane?"

"What?"

"They don't know about it, do they?" she said.

"No, and I intend to keep it that way. They have all the others, and this one isn't going to reveal some major clue that they just have to know."

She held her hand out, and I gave her the note.

"Well I, for one, applaud you," she said. "You know me; I'm all about going rogue. Does anyone else know about this?"

"Giovanni."

"How?" she said.

"You can add that to all the other mysteries of the universe that I haven't solved about him. I have no idea how he knew, he just did."

"So where'd you get this?" she said.

I told her.

"I can't believe you found it like that," she said. "What a fluke."

"He knew I would," I said. "It's like he knows how I think—how I work. It's almost like he's in my head, and I can't get him out."

CHAPTER 24

Two hours later I was in front of the counter inside The Pretty Pen, an old-fashioned shop in a weathered stucco building decorated on the inside in painted stripes the color of milk chocolate and baby blue. I frequented it often since they peddled two of my favorite things—books and customized stationery.

A black-haired boy was hunched over the opposite side of the counter with his eyes glued to a page in a Stephen King novel. His hair had been shaped with great attention and a lot of grease, and he had holes in his ears the size of nickels. When he shifted positions and leaned over the counter, I got a peephole view of the shelf of books on the wall behind him. It was like looking through a magnifying glass without any magnification. After a minute or two, it became clear that he either didn't see me or he didn't care, and my patience was spent.

"Excuse me," I said.

He made an upward whipping motion with his head in my direction, but his hair didn't move an inch.

"What's up?" he said, or tried to say. Given the fact that he mumbled the words under his breath, I couldn't be sure.

"Robert around?" I said.

"Yeah, but he's chillin' in the back right now with like some boxes of books that came in and I think he's busy with that so he told me to come out here and help the customers."

The operative word being help, as in to actually offer assistance when needed.

"Can you just tell him Sloane is here? He knows me."

"Oh uh, I dunno. He said not to bother him, and he gets kinda mad when I do, so…"

I crossed to the other side of the counter and walked toward the back room. The kid seemed put off by this and shouted after me.

"You can't go back there," he said.

"No worries," I said, and I pushed open the partition that separated the main part of the store from the back room.

A voice from the back sounded off.

"Dammit Kyle, I told you not to—"

"Kyle's still up front," I said. "It's just me, Robert."

The man poked his head around one of the boxes and

looked up at me.

"Oh Sloane. How are you?" he said.

He grabbed a paper towel from the green Formica countertop next to him and wiped his hands off and then stood up.

"I hope you don't mind me coming back here," I said.

He swished the air in a downward motion with his hand.

"Naw," he said. "You're my best customer."

"Who's the new kid?" I said.

He rolled his eyes.

"My nephew. I promised my sister I'd give him a job for the summer. He's only here for another five days or so."

"Sounds like you're counting them down," I said.

"You have no idea. I'd pay him not to come in at this point."

"Wow, that bad, huh?"

"I got what you asked for."

"Really?" I said. "You found it?"

"It wasn't easy, but I sure did. Come over here and take a look."

I followed him over to his desk. He opened the drawer and pulled out a big piece of cloth and set it in my hands. I unfolded it and stared in wonderment at the book before me.

"Well," he said. "What do you think?"

"I can't believe you were able to find one in such good condition," I said. "I've dreamed about owning this for years."

"Sorry it took so long to procure it for you," he said.

"Don't be. It was worth the wait."

In my hand I held a UK first edition copy of Agatha Christie's first novel *The Mysterious Affair at Styles.* I'd collected her works for years and always hoped one day I would be able to afford the first book she ever wrote.

"It's too bad I wasn't around when it first came out," I said. "I would only owe you seven shillings and sixpence."

He laughed.

"You missed that by a good ninety-some years, I'd say."

I wrapped the cloth back around the book and placed it in the protective case it came in.

"I need to ask a favor," I said.

"Another book?"

I shook my head.

"This is far more important," I said.

I reached in my bag and lowered my volume to a whisper.

"I need you to take a look at this," I said.

Robert withdrew the pink paper from my hands and held it flat on his palm while he walked over to his desk and put his glasses on. He held it a few inches from his face and scrutinized every part of it without uttering a word. After some time, he glanced up at me.

"May I ask you something?" he said.

"Anything."

"Is this for a case you're working on?"

"It is. Can I count on you to be discreet?" I said.

"You don't even need to ask."

"I was hoping you'd say that," I said.

"What is it you would like me to do?"

"Is there anything you can tell me about it?" I said.

"Well, it appears to be made of parchment of some kind."

He took his fingers and grazed them across the top.

"And this ripped part at the top here," he said, "it's called a deckle edge."

"Do you have any idea who makes it or where it came from?" I said.

"I don't carry this in the store, but I may be able to find it. Leave me a piece of it, and I'll see what I can find out for you."

CHAPTER 25

I stood in front of the wall at my office and pinned up three-quarters of the last note Sinnerman left for me to his profile board. I stared at it and tried to focus on what my next move would be, but all I could think about was Giovanni. Every time he was around it clouded my judgment, and now, with him nowhere in sight, it was even worse. My concentration was off.

The night before I'd spent a lot of time wrapped up in my thoughts about Giovanni's request to work together. Under most circumstances, I didn't want help, and I never asked for it. It was odd to me that I considered allowing someone in my world when I knew so little of his.

When my grandfather was alive, he taught me the importance of what he liked to call "the power of observation." He said most people reveal themselves when they don't think anyone else is watching, and in those moments you can truly unravel their essence and learn what they're made of and why they do the things they do. I'd taken his advice to heart.

In my life I'd formed my own circle of trust, and the circle was small. To let someone in required time and plenty of observation on my part. I'd made it a point never to show my cards until they'd shown theirs. I watched and I waited until they exposed themselves to me. This method was flawless until the day Giovanni Luciana stepped into my life, and I found I wanted to show my hand before he even decided to call or wager.

CHAPTER 26

Sam Reids stood behind a paisley curtain in a window of an office that was desolate except for a chair he'd brought in when he didn't want to stand. Sloane had a puzzled look on her face, and he wondered why and what her thoughts were in that moment. *Is she thinking of me*, he thought. A warm sensation flushed up and down his arms at the very thought of it.

Sam adjusted his binoculars and directed his attention to the most recent addition to the board, the pink slip of paper. *Clever girl*, he thought, *keeping that one all to yourself.* He knew it wouldn't lead her any closer to him. Still, he enjoyed looking at the visual remnants of his crimes attached to the cork board on her wall. It gave him a sense of pride, a sense that he belonged in some odd way. Like he mattered, even if her motive was to ultimately end his life. He was sure in time she'd come to see things in a different way.

Sloane wasn't like most women; she was fearless, like he was. Maybe that was the reason he'd grown so fond of her. Of all his adversaries, she proved the most worthy. It was fun to leave her little crumbs and tidbits here and there and then to sit back and watch her find them. He wanted to test her, to see if they rattled her, and he was surprised when they didn't. She reminded him of a curious puppy after a certain scent. The question was, would she get a good whiff of it? He didn't think so, although to underestimate her wouldn't be wise, so he kept tabs on her just like he was doing now from an office across the street from her own.

The game he played with Sloane had been fun, but now Sam wanted to go in a different direction. His patience waned, and he was ready to reward himself for his efforts. He felt he deserved it, and he knew what he needed to do. The time had come to see what Sloane Monroe was made of and to let the fireworks begin. His most recent two had gone off, and he was ready for the grand finale. The moment where he would secure the best, the one he saved for last.

CHAPTER 27

My cell phone rang. It was Giovanni.

"My brother would like you to come down to the station," he said.

"Did he say why?"

"Are you sitting down?" he said.

"Should I be?"

"You should," he said. "I'll wait."

I paused about five seconds for good measure and continued to apply my makeup. He wasn't there and would never know the difference.

"Ready," I said.

"They have someone in custody."

My mascara wand plummeted from my hand and streaked the left side of my cheek before it settled in the center of the sink.

"Dammit," I said.

"You weren't sitting, were you?"

"When you said they had someone in custody, you didn't mean they think this guy is Sinnerman, right?"

"That's precisely what I meant."

"Tell him I'll be there in thirty minutes."

*****

Twenty-nine minutes later I made my entrance.

"How are you doing today?" Rose said when I approached the front desk.

"Ask me again in a few minutes," I said.

"That Agent Luciana guy told me to have you wait out here for a few minutes and then they will call you back."

"Did you get a look at him?" I said. "The guy they brought in?"

"He had his face covered when he got here so I didn't see much."

"And has anyone said anything about him since he's been here?"

"Not a word."

"Who brought him in?" I said.

"Coop."

I nodded and took a seat in a section of chairs that rested along the wall opposite the reception desk. Three chairs over from me sat a female who hadn't looked up since I walked in. Her long hair was the color of the inside of a banana and was loosely tied with a rubber band, the kind you get from a newspaper. One of the strands of hair had fallen in her face and she fiddled with it—putting it in her mouth and taking it back out again. Her clothes were dirty, and her jeans which were a few sizes too big, looked like they'd just slid into home plate.

After we sat for a few minutes in silence, she lifted her head just enough that I caught a partial glimpse of her face. There was some puffiness around her left eye, and she had a diagonal cut that ran a couple of inches across her cheekbone.

"Are you okay?" I said.

"You the person I'm supposed to talk to?"

"Did your boyfriend do that to you?"

She rolled her eyes.

"Some idiot did this to me, and when I find out who he is I'm going to—"

"What happened?" I said.

"If I tell you, you'll help me right? You'll catch the guy?"

"I'm not a cop," I said.

"Who are you then?"

"I'm a private investigator."

"I need a cop."

I shrugged.

"Fine by me. I bet I can catch him in half the time, but do what you think is best."

We sat in silence for a couple more minutes and then

she said, "Could you really? I mean, are you that good?"

"I am," I said.

For whatever reason, I had an extra boost of confidence today.

The girl stood up from her chair and looked over at Rose, who appeared to be minding her own business, but we both knew she wasn't, and then she sat down in the chair next to me.

"My name's Trisha," she said.

"Sloane."

"You been a PI for long?"

"I have."

"And do you always catch the bad guy?" she said.

"About ninety-nine percent of the time."

"And the other one percent?" she said.

"I'm working on that one right now."

She gave me a look to indicate her confusion but didn't say anything.

"So what happened to you?" I said.

"I took my beagle out for a walk this morning, and this guy comes out of nowhere and just starts up a conversation with me. So we're going back and forth about where we live and how long we'd lived there, and I look down at my dog, and the next thing I know the guy grabs me, and he's got a rock, and he's about to smash the side of my head with it. I let go of the leash, and he wrestled me to the ground and when he raised his hand to strike, I clocked him. Right in the eye. Then I grabbed my dog and ran like hell."

I found it interesting that she claimed she attacked him since she was the one with the shiner.

"Where were you assaulted?"

"Right in my own neighborhood, if you can believe that. The nerve of the guy—it was like eight o'clock in the morning."

"Today?"

She nodded.

"Did you get a good look at him?" I said.

"He had his face shielded with a—"

"Lemme guess," I said. "Hoodie."

"How'd you know?"

"Let's just say I've heard that word a lot this week," I said.

"I'd recognize him if I saw him again though. He was about my height and had a certain way that he walked, like one of his legs was longer than the other or something. It was weird."

I reached into my bag and pulled out a tissue and handed it to her.

"What's this for?"

"Your nose," I said. "It's bleeding."

She glanced down and a drop of blood dripped from her nose and splotched on the white flecked vinyl tiles on the floor. She snatched the tissue from my hand and turned away.

"There's a bathroom through those doors to your right," I said.

The woman nodded and stood up and made a beeline for the ladies' room. When she returned, I advised her to talk to the cops and then gave her my card and asked her to come by my office the following day.

The conference room door opened, and Coop walked out with various other men who I suspected were part of Agent Luciana's minions. There was no sign of Giovanni or his brother and no sign of Nick either. Coop looked my way for a brief moment and then spun around like he hadn't seen me, even though it was obvious he did.

Another minute went by and the chief walked out of the room followed by a man in handcuffs and Agent Luciana, who rounded out the back.

Trisha bolted out the bathroom door and seized my arm with her hand.

"That's him!" she said.

"Him who?" I said.

She pointed in the direction of the man in cuffs.

"That's the guy who attacked me!"

Before I could form any words she was halfway across the room and on a mission. Coop spotted her and made a move to tackle her like he was going for a first and ten, but he was about two seconds too late. She slipped past him and raised her hand into the air and slapped the cuffed guy across the face. And for the first time since exiting the room, he raised his head, but his eyes didn't meet hers, they met mine. For a few moments it was like time stood still, and the only two people in the room were him and me. Trisha spewed all sorts of expletives while Coop and the chief tried to keep her at bay, but I couldn't hear any of it. It was like someone hit the mute button in the room, and our eyes remained locked in some sort of a trance, and I had only one thing on my mind: Was I looking into the face of my sister's killer?

Someone touched my shoulder, and I jerked back.

"It's just me," the voice said.

Sound returned to the room and my eyes settled on Giovanni, who stood next to me with a look of genuine concern on his face. I flipped back around, but Agent Luciana had ushered the guy almost all the way out of the room. Before they traveled through the doorway into the hall, the man turned and glanced at me once more. He had the strangest expression on his face, and it threw me off.

I turned to Trisha who was still clutched tight within Coop and the chief's firm grip.

"That is the guy from this morning?" I said.

She nodded.

"What is she talking about?" the chief said.

With Trisha shaken up over being presented with a

visual of her aggressor, I gave him a brief summary of what she'd just told me.

When I finished he turned to Trisha and said, "Are you sure?"

Coop and the chief loosened their grip but advised her not to make a move.

"Of course I'm sure," she said. "That was him."

*****

The chief put Trisha in a room with a couple of his guys and then whisked me over to his office. Giovanni waited outside. I wasn't sure if he was there for his brother or for me.

"What in the world is going on?" I said. "Is it really him?"

The chief sighed.

"This morning we got a tip from someone who said they saw a guy that matched the description of our sketch. Man said it was his neighbor. We've received tons of calls like this. Difference is, when we got to this schmuck's house to question him, we found all kinds of evidence in his car."

"What kind of evidence?" I said.

"He had Polaroid photos of the last two victims in plain sight on the passenger seat of his car, and we also found two different strands of hair, which we're running now." The chief looked me in the eye. "I know this is hard

Sloane, but it looks like we got him."

I didn't know what to say.

"I'm sure you're in shock," the chief said. "No one can blame you for that."

"I don't know," I said. "It's not that. I need to think. I suppose I can't see him?"

The chief shook his head.

"It wouldn't do you much good anyway; he hasn't said much to us since we picked him up."

"What has he said?"

"Two words. I'm innocent."

CHAPTER 28

After I finished with the chief Giovanni met up with me
in the hall.

"Dinner?"

"I'm exhausted," I said. "But thank you."

"Some other time then?"

I nodded and made some lame excuse about how I
had to leave. I needed to be alone tonight.

*****

I arrived home, changed into a tank top and some grey
yoga pants, and then fell back on my bed. With my
thumb and pointer finger, I rubbed my temples in a
circular motion. Lord Berkeley hopped up on the bed
with his miniature-sized tennis ball in his mouth and
dropped it three inches or so from my hand and rolled it
over the rest of the way with his nose.

"Not tonight, Boo," I said. "Mommy has to think."

He looked at me, and I imagined if he could have

frowned, he would have. After a couple minutes of staring me down, he decided I wasn't going to budge and opted for the next best thing—he curled up next to me and took a nap. I stroked his white fur and closed my eyes. The cuffed man's face was still ingrained in my mind, and I imagined it would remain that way forever. He looked different than I thought he would, and I didn't know how to feel about that.

I remembered back to a time before I'd started dating Nick, when Maddie, tired of seeing me alone, felt the incessant urge to sign me up on a dating site on the Internet. Resistance was futile, and after several months had gone by, I agreed to correspond by email with a guy named Charles David. He only had a couple of profile pictures posted on the site and one was blurry, but the other—his main photo—drew me in. His hair was ash blond and fell to both sides of his face in a perfect wave just like a Ken doll, and his blue eyes reminded me of the water in the Bahamas. But what hooked me was his smile. It was the kind of smile a person could look at forever. We emailed for a couple weeks until I was brave enough to meet. I set the time and place, and while I sat at the restaurant and waited, I tried my best to quell the nerves inside me. And then it was time. He walked in dressed in a white polo shirt just like he said he'd have on and a pair of jeans. But there was just one problem. He didn't look a thing like the Charles David in the photo, and after a couple minutes of interrogation, he admitted the picture was of his brother—his married brother, Simon David. And that put an end to our date and my stint at online dating.

I thought back to the guy I'd seen today, the alleged Sinnerman. When we locked eyes, I was shocked to find they didn't look like the eyes of a killer. They weren't evil, like I thought they'd be—they were scared, and for a brief moment, terrified. He looked more like a child who'd just been caught stealing a piece of candy at the grocery store and worried what kind of trouble he was going to be in when the store manager called his parents.

And there was something else that bothered me: his stature. He walked with a slight limp, and I wasn't sure why, and he had a tiny frame, almost smaller than that of a woman. He looked like a lightweight, and I couldn't imagine he weighed more than a hundred fifty-five pounds. At that size, it was hard for me to believe he had the power to overtake one woman, let alone several.

I was jostled out of my thoughts by the sound of Lord Berkeley sprinting off the bed when my doorbell rang. I squeezed my eyes open and closed a few times to bring myself back to life and then reached for my nine millimeter on the nightstand.

I advanced down the hall to the door and shouted, "Who's there?"

"It's me. Just wanted to see how you were doing."

I opened the door, and Giovanni presented me with the most beautiful arrangement of flowers I'd ever seen.

He eyed my gun and then my dog, who flashed his entire set of pearly whites.

"9mm, nice choice. You pick that out yourself?"

I nodded and invited him inside.

"I'm doing fine," I said. "Any news?"

He shook his head.

"These are beautiful," I said, and pointed to the plant with purple flowers he'd just given me. "What are they?"

"Aquilegia vulgaris."

"I didn't know you could get flowers like this around here," I said.

He grinned.

"You can't."

"Do you want to sit down?" I said.

"I can't stay, but I'm glad to see you're doing so well."

I found it odd that he drove all the way over just to assess my wellness.

"Do you know about the summer concert series here in town?" he said.

"I go every year."

"Tomorrow night, they have a great lineup. I purchased tickets for the two of us."

"I don't know," I said. "So much is happening right now with the case and everything and things have developed so fast that I should—"

"That's why this is the perfect escape. You need a night away from this where you can sit back and unwind and take your mind off everything."

I didn't want to admit it, but he was right. Giovanni smiled at Lord Berkeley and extended his hand out to him. Lord Berkeley snapped his jaw together in response. I scooped him up and excused myself and shut him in the bedroom.

"It's not a good idea to try and pet him until he knows you," I said.

Giovanni nodded.

"I'll keep that in mind," he said. "Pick you up at seven tomorrow night?"

"See you then."

CHAPTER 29

Months with warm weather were my favorite, and summer in Park City was no exception. Skiers had packed up and gone home to await the next season, and the town was replaced with cyclists, golfers, and those who enjoyed the warm weather and the great outdoors, and that group included me. On Wednesdays, the Farmer's Market lured both residents and seasonal visitors with its wide array of locally grown fruits and vegetables and other novelties. And then there was the annual food and wine festival in July which lasted four days and celebrated at the end with a night of jazz, food from some of the best local restaurants in town, and wine tasting. But one of my favorite events was the summer concert series held at one of the local ski resorts, and tonight I would take my spot on the lawn alongside Giovanni and partake of the cool, summer breeze Park City had to offer.

I selected a summery black tank dress for the evening

and low peep-toe heels. Giovanni arrived on time and had forgone the suit, and for the first time since we met, he was dressed in designer jeans and a fitted polo shirt. I always had the impression he was on the slender side: but the shirt showed off something I hadn't expected, a toned physique that hadn't been shaped overnight. It was a different side of him, and I expected it was one of many.

"You look beautiful," he said when we arrived at the car.

I reached for the handle.

"Let me get that for you," he said.

I smiled and waited like a high school girl on her first date for him to advance around the side of the car and open my door. There was no way I could ever get used to him holding the car door open for me; it was just too weird.

*****

The grassy area surrounding the outdoor amphitheater was littered with blankets and picnic baskets packed with a wide array of items from tea sandwiches to bottles of wine. Everyone seemed content just to be there to take in such a perfect night.

"I should have brought a blanket," I said. "I don't know what I was thinking. I walked out the door and forgot all about it."

Giovanni turned and smiled at me with his usual laid

back attitude and then extended his right hand out with his palm up.

"Here we are," he said.

On the grass in front of us was an entire set up—a blanket had been spread out, and in the middle of it was an open basket full of food and wine. He'd thought of everything.

"I see you went ahead," I said.

"I had someone take care of this earlier," he said. "Does this work for you?"

We were in the exact center of the lawn about a quarter up from the stage with a perfect view of the amphitheater.

I nodded.

Right before the first act came out, Giovanni reached into the basket next to him and pulled out two glasses.

"Red or white wine?" he said. "I wasn't sure, so I brought both."

"Red."

He nodded and poured.

"I'd like to know more about you," he said.

"I was thinking the same thing about you."

"Ladies first."

"All right then," I said. "Ask away."

"Have you always lived here?"

"Not always. I grew up in a small town in California."

"Why move?"

"My grandfather lived here. When I was a kid, I spent my summers in Park City with my sister."

"Gabrielle?"

I nodded.

"She was my only sibling," I said. "It was always just the two of us. After I graduated, I came out for a visit and decided to stay, and I've been here ever since. Gabby stayed in California for a while, and then joined me here about five years ago."

"Ever marry?"

"Once," I said.

"Hmm."

"We were young," I said. "Too young. And so different from each other. At the time I thought he was everything I could ask for in a person, but when I look back now, I realize I couldn't have known what I wanted at the time. He saw things one way, and I saw things in another, and the two didn't coincide. But even then, it was hard for me to walk away."

"Why do you think that is?"

"When I commit to something or someone," I said, "I'm all in, and it's hard for me to back down, even when I know it's the right thing to do."

"But you did."

I took a sip of wine, but what I really wanted was to grab the bottle and polish it off in one long swallow. It wasn't easy for me to open up, and I was miles away from my comfort zone, but if I expected him to reciprocate, I knew I had to offer something.

"He started drinking," I said. "At first it was just a few beers here and there, but the months forged on, and January turned into June, until one day he was a full-blown alcoholic."

"Do you know what caused him to get that way?"

"Some days I thought it was me," I said.

Giovanni's hand grazed my knee.

"I doubt that."

"He wanted kids. I think he thought kids would solve our problems, and maybe if I got pregnant, I wouldn't leave."

"And you didn't?"

"I've always wanted children; it's just that I haven't been able to…"

What was I doing? I'd divulged more to Giovanni in a couple hours than I had with Nick in three years together.

"How did it end?"

"At the time I wanted to follow in my grandfather's footsteps and join the FBI, and I was taking steps to begin that process, and he didn't approve. He actually told me he wouldn't stand for it, like my life was at his discretion. It was too much. I left, and I never went back."

"And now?"

"I live life on my terms."

He grinned and shook his head.

"I meant to say, how is your relationship with Detective Calhoun?"

Somehow I knew he would come up.

"Hard to explain," I said.

"But you do have one?"

"Had," I said. "I ended it about a week ago."

It was all I wanted to say on the subject. Giovanni was quiet for several moments before he spoke again.

"I never thought Detective Calhoun was the right man for you."

How could he possibly know whether he is or isn't?

"Ah, I can tell from the look on your face I've offended you," he said. "I'm sorry."

"Don't be," I said. "It's just that you hardly know me. Nick isn't such a bad guy. I'm just at a point in my life where I…"

What was it with me tonight? In one evening I'd turned into Chatty Cathy.

"When I look at you I see an independent woman, one who doesn't take no for an answer. Someone who never backs down from a challenge. You're as passionate about the cases you take on as the clients you work for. You like being in a relationship, but you don't need it to survive. Would you like me to go on?"

I wanted to say something, but what, I didn't know. He continued.

"I believe what happened to your sister affected you in a profound way, and that you've never gotten past it, even though you've tried. Somehow you've persuaded yourself to believe that once you catch the killer, things will change, but deep down you know it will never bring you the peace of mind you long for. There will always be a void in your life, a hole incapable of closing up. I too have lost the people I love—those closest to me. You learn to live with it, move on, and you do because you have to. But the pain doesn't ever go away, not all of it."

There was a time when I thought Nick knew me so well, but no one had ever come close to what I'd experienced with Giovanni in such a short amount of time. I looked around and noticed everyone started to clap and had stood up and gathered their blankets, and I realized the concert was already over. I stood with Giovanni and then bent down and grabbed a corner of the blanket.

He placed his hand on my wrist. "Leave it," he said. "Someone else will take care of it."

The drive home was spent in an uncomfortable silence, for me anyway. Giovanni seemed content and had a permanent smile on his face for the entire ride. I couldn't help but wonder what he thought of my over-share, and I was surprised I'd reminisced over a past I tried hard to forget. Once again I came away with little more information about Giovanni than I already knew about him. It was a disappointment.

We reached my house, and Giovanni shut the car off and reclined back in his seat and gazed at me, which gave me the impression he wanted to continue our little chat. I didn't.

"I need to say something," I said.

"Go on."

"I know it's a sign of respect to open the door for a woman, but it's too much. Please don't take it the wrong way, but I can manage my own door from now on." And with that, I opened the car door and got out and closed it behind me.

Now what?

Giovanni exited his side of the car, and when I turned to see how he'd taken what I just said, his hand was over his mouth and all I could see was his backside.

"Are you laughing at me?" I said.

"I'm sorry."

"What's so funny?" I said.

"You are."

"In what way?"

"You are so different."

"What's that supposed to mean?" I said.

"I've never met another woman quite like you."

We walked up the path that led to my front porch, and when I glanced in his direction, he still had a look of amusement on his face. I reached for the door and turned.

"What is it that you want from me?" I said.

He cupped his hand beneath my chin and leaned in and stared into my eyes for a moment and then gave me a kiss, but not on the lips—on the cheek of all places, which made me feel like I'd just bid a fond farewell to my brother, if I had one.

"See you tomorrow," he said.

CHAPTER 30

"He kissed you?"

I nodded.

"If you can call it a kiss."

I felt like a teenager who couldn't wait to give the scoop to her girlfriend.

"And what did you do?" Maddie said.

"I'm not sure, it all happened kinda fast."

Maddie and I had just finished jujitsu class and were on our way to her lab. Her eyes were lit up like a sparkler on the Fourth of July.

"Well, did you kiss him back or what?" she said.

"On his cheek? Wouldn't that seem a bit strange?"

She popped a bubble with the green, apple-flavored gum she swished around inside her mouth.

"Girl, you should have slid your face over a few inches and gone in for the real deal. You know he wouldn't have said no."

"I imagine one day our lips will make a connection and when they do it will be *first-prize-at-the-fair* good."

She smacked me on the shoulder, tossed her head back and laughed.

"Good for you," she said. "I can tell you're looking forward to it."

"You don't think it's a big deal?"

She shrugged. "Why would it be?"

"I just got out of a relationship a week ago, Maddie. Shouldn't I feel bad or something?"

"Why, because you think it's too soon?" she said.

"Isn't it?"

"If he did kiss you, or tried something more—would you regret it?"

I shook my head.

"Well then, there's your answer," she said.

"Maybe you're right."

"I need to meet this guy though. Then I can tell you how I really feel."

We arrived at the lab and went in. Maddie walked over to her desk and opened a file.

"Okay, this is what I wanted to show you," she said.

"What am I looking at?"

"Hair follicles."

"These were found in the suspect's car, right?"

She nodded.

"They're an exact match to the last two victims," she

said.

"I can't believe it."

"It proves they were both in his car."

"So we have our killer?"

"Maybe."

"What do you mean?"

"When I took a close look at the hair found in the car, I noticed something unusual," she said. "It's just a minor thing—but it's been on my mind. Usually when hair is found like that, it's a secondary transfer."

"Meaning?"

"A piece has fallen out on its own and attached itself to whatever is there—the seat, fibers in the carpet, a floor mat, etc. If the hair falls out naturally, the root has a club shape which is easy for me to see. If the killer yanked it out on the other hand, the root is stretched and sometimes broken. Neither applies to the strands of hair I tested."

"Are you suggesting they might have been planted?" I said.

"All I know is, both strands of hair had been cut like scissors were used to remove the individual pieces."

"He never did that with any of his victims. Why would he start now, and why leave just a few strands of cut hair in the car? That's sloppy and careless; it's not like him at all."

CHAPTER 31

I left the lab and placed a call to Giovanni.

"I need a favor," I said.

"Name it."

"I want the address of the guy they have in custody for the Sinnerman murders."

"You heard the news then?"

"I just left Maddie's lab," I said.

"Can you hold on a minute?"

After holding a short time, Giovanni returned to the line.

"Five twenty-five Spruce Street," he said. "In some condos. Number nine. Should I ask why you want it?"

"Better if you didn't."

I thanked him and ended the call. By now I was sure everyone at the station had broken out the champagne to celebrate the capture of Sinnerman. But even with the evidence stacked a mile high against him, I had to be sure.

*****

The door at five twenty-five Spruce Street #9 was unlocked, which was convenient, and at present no one was there. I expected forensics had already come and gone, along with Park City's finest. I knocked just in case he had roommates or a wife, but no one answered, so I went in. The living room was cluttered with all kinds of newspapers, magazines, and wadded-up computer paper that rested on the cheap, blue, plush carpet.

In the corner of the room was a fish tank. From the looks of it, the tank hadn't been cleaned in a while. A guppie floated upside down at the top. The walls in the room were adorned with posters from what I presumed were his favorite bands: the Grateful Dead, the Doors, and the Rolling Stones. The sink in the kitchen was full of dishes with hardened food stuck to them, and when I opened the fridge, it was barren except for a couple beers and a few to go boxes.

I felt a strange sensation in my leg and jerked back. A fluffy, grey cat the width of three average-sized cats leapt onto the counter and eyed me curiously. I reached over and lifted her off the counter and stroked her thick fur. "What's your name then?" I said. She nuzzled up against me and purred, and then I released her back on the floor. She turned and walked down the hall toward a bedroom. I followed. It was the only other room in the house besides a Cracker Jack-sized bathroom. The queen-sized bed was hoisted up on a set of cinder blocks, but there was no comforter of any kind, only grey sheets and a single black blanket. A stack of comic books offered the only sign of organization in the entire house.

Overall the place was trashed. The guy lived like a hermit with almost no possessions to speak of which made me wonder: if he liked to take Polaroid pictures of the women, where was the camera? And what about the little mementos he kept? As grisly as they were, there was no sign anyone had ever been brought here. Could he have taken the women somewhere else? And what if it wasn't him? Why did he have photos of the women in his car…and their hair—and how did it get there?

CHAPTER 32

Giovanni stood in the corner of the room in my office. With his pointer finger and thumb he stroked his chin a few times and eyed the shrine to Sinnerman on my wall.

"Quite the collection you have here. You've been at it awhile."

"I created it a few weeks after my sister died," I said.

"I can imagine how much this means to you, and I'm grateful you felt comfortable enough to share it with me."

I rose from the chair at my desk and walked over and stood next to him.

"I wanted you to see this because of what I am about to tell you. Let's just say I have my doubts anyone will believe me, but I thought if I had you in my corner—"

"Go on."

"I'm not sure the right man is in custody," I said.

"Even after the evidence they found?"

I nodded.

"I've been to his house, and something doesn't add up," I said. "It was a wreck, and from the profile I created of Sinnerman and what we know of him, I believe he's organized, almost to a fault. This guy's not, by miles. Plus, I looked into his eyes just before they locked him up. Giovanni, they're not the eyes of a killer."

He absorbed what I had to say and then looked at me for a moment to make sure I had finished. I hadn't.

"He doesn't make mistakes," I said. "His crimes are orchestrated in such a perfect way that never once has he left behind any indication of who he is: not a print, not a drop of blood, nada. Until now we've had no indication about who this guy is, and yet I'm expected to believe within a twenty-four hour period, a killer who always covers his tracks leaves evidence in his car that his neighbor just happens to find? And then attacks a woman in broad daylight who gets the best of him, yet he still manages to flee the scene?"

"Do you know what first attracted me to you?" he said.

This caught me off guard. I brought him to my office to discuss Sinnerman, not feelings.

He continued. "You're bright. You take the time to look at things from all angles. You see the things others can't and go far beyond the evidence presented to you. Most people only scratch the surface, but not you. And that's a rare quality in anyone."

"Do you believe me?"

"I believe *in* you."

The conversation had taken a turn for the awkward, to say the least. I'd never been great at being showered with compliments. To make it even more intense, he hadn't taken his eyes off me. It threw me off balance. He seemed to sense this and said, "What can I do to put your mind at ease?"

I smiled. Now we were getting somewhere.

*****

A short time later, I sat on a cheap tan metal chair in a dingy, grey room devoid of adornment of any kind. The man accused of the Sinnerman murders sat across from me. I gazed at him, and he stared down into his lap. Even though he didn't look at me, I could tell he was scared. His face was pale, his shoulder blades were arched inward, and his frame was weak, like someone who hadn't slept for days. From what I'd been told, he hadn't spoken to anyone except his lawyer, and his lawyer had yet to make a statement.

"Do you know who I am?" I said.

He didn't flinch.

"You should. You've written me several notes, remember?"

Silence.

"No? Let's see if I can jog your memory then," I said.

I reached into my pocket and pulled out a slip of paper and slid it over to him.

"Recognize it?"

His eyes scanned the paper, but he didn't move. I gave him a moment and then reached over and took it back. Now that I had his attention, or at least some of it, I upped the ante. With my pointer finger, I inched a photo over to him. And we had movement. He glanced at it and shuddered, then shielded his face with his cuffed hands. Just like I thought he would.

"That's a picture of my sister," I said. "Taken right after her body was found."

"Get it away from me," he said.

I reached over and flipped the photo around to the other side.

"Is that better?" I said.

He nodded and looked up at me, flashing his sweet baby-blues. "Thank you."

I nodded but didn't utter a word. I hoped he would talk. He didn't. I waited.

A few minutes went by and he said, "I saw you at the station the other day. You a cop?"

I shook my head.

"Why are you here then?" he said. "Is it because of your sister?"

I nodded.

He looked around the room like he was afraid

someone would eavesdrop on our back-and-forth banter, which was an accurate assumption, and then leaned in toward me.

"I'm sorry about your sister," he said. "I don't know how her hair got in my car. I swear I don't. But I didn't do it. I've never hurt anyone."

I slouched back in my chair and closed my eyes and breathed. When I opened them, I said, "I know you didn't do it. I don't know if I could sit across from you like this if you did."

He shifted his eyes, and they reflected something I hadn't seen in them before—hope.

"Wait—what?" he said.

"The photo I showed you of my sister was taken over three years ago, and her hair wasn't found in your car. It was hair from the two most recent victims. Tell me something," I said, "if you're innocent, and I believe you are, why haven't you said anything to the cops?"

"I was afraid I'd say the wrong thing, and just make it worse."

"How much worse can it get?"

"Maybe you're right," he said. "But my lawyer said not to talk unless he was present, so I didn't. Besides, I didn't think anyone would listen to me anyway. They all think I did it."

"What do you know about the case?" I said.

"Not much. I only moved here about six months

ago."

"Is there any reason why someone would frame you for the murders?"

He shook his head.

"I don't even know many people here yet. I haven't been here long enough to make enemies, not that I do anyway."

"Why did you move here?" I said.

"I got a waiter position at a new restaurant in town."

"Seems like a long way to go to be a waiter."

He shook his head.

"You don't understand. One of the best chefs in the country works here, and he said he'd let me work under him on my days off."

"What's your name?" I said.

"Ryan Saunders."

I stood. "Well, Ryan Saunders, my name is Sloane. Let me see what I can do to help you."

"What makes you think you can?"

I grabbed the door and turned the knob. I looked back at him.

"Watch and see."

CHAPTER 33

Giovanni and his brother were in the hall when I exited the room. His brother wasn't smiling.

"He didn't do it," I said. "He doesn't fit the profile, and if you studied it long enough, you'd know it too."

Agent Luciana wasn't amused.

"Lots of serials don't fit the profile; that doesn't mean it's not him," Agent Luciana said.

"I'm telling you, this guy isn't the killer. He just about catapulted off his chair when I showed him Gabrielle's picture."

"I know, I saw," Agent Luciana said.

"Then you're aware of how inconsistent that is from typical behavior. Put this photo in front a serial killer, and he won't even flinch. He'd lean in for a closer look and then ask to keep it."

"Or it's all just an act."

"Nothing about it seemed staged to me."

"Doesn't mean it wasn't," Agent Luciana said.

"Lock him away then," I said. "And when the real killer strikes again, and he will, don't call me to help you cover your ass."

"You're overstepping," Agent Luciana said.

"And you can't see what's right in front of your face."

"So maybe the guy didn't kill your sister. That still doesn't account for the hair and the photos that were found in his car."

"Easy," I said. "They were planted. It's happened before."

Giovanni, who up until that time seemed amused by the exchange, turned toward his brother and placed his hand on his shoulder.

"If she says it's not him Carlo, I believe her."

"Since when do you let a woman cloud your judgment Gio?" Agent Luciana said.

"Never," Giovanni replied.

CHAPTER 34

Sam Reids watched the news on the television unfold. A reporter announced a man had been arrested and was being held for questioning in the Sinnerman murders. Sam was delighted by this and proud of his latest coup. Everything had worked out just the way he wanted—of course. He relished the thought of it all and hoped tomorrow would afford him the opportunity he needed to secure his grand prize. In the meantime, he needed to tend to a different matter.

Sam climbed into his car, revved the engine a few times, and drove six miles away to the local gas station. It was dark out, but in the pale glow of the street light, he could make out her frail frame blending with the shadows of the monstrous trees next to her.

"Took you long enough," she said when he exited the car.

He glared at her but didn't speak.

"You got my money?" she said.

Sam lifted his wallet from his back pocket, opened it, and took out a series of bills and held them out to the woman. She stared down at the money he presented to her with a foolish grin on her face. The money called out to her like the drugs she couldn't resist, and she didn't fight it. All she wanted to do was grab it and stuff it inside her leopard-patterned bra. She reached her hand out and wrapped it around the top of the bills. Sam tightened his grip on the money.

"What gives?" she said.

In a whisper, he replied. "First I want to know how the other day went."

"I did what you said."

He gripped the money tighter.

"Details."

"All right, fine. I went to the station at the time you told me to, and when the guy came out of the room with those cops all cuffed and everything, I told them he was the one who attacked me. And then they had me come into a room and give them a statement."

"And did they believe you?"

"The vultures ate up every word of it," she said.

"Anything else?"

She shook her head.

"And the cops were the only ones you spoke to?" Sam said.

"Just one other person, but it wasn't a big deal."

Sam's nostrils flared. He balled both hands into fists but was careful not to strike.

Through gritted teeth he said, "I told you not to speak to anyone else."

"There wasn't nothin' I could do about it. She just started talking to me and wouldn't shut up."

"*She*—who?"

"Some woman who sat by me in the waiting room before all the drama went down. Said her name was Simone, I think."

Sam felt his body temperature fluctuate, and a sensation of hot and then cold coarsed through his veins. His face perspired, and tiny beads of moisture seeped from his hands.

"Was it Sloane?"

"Oh hey yeah, that was it," she said. "How'd you know?"

Sam sealed his eyes shut and tried to suppress the rage building inside his body. He thought about how nice it would be to kill her—right then, right there. But after a moment, he assured himself that it didn't matter. Sloane wouldn't be able to figure things out—she couldn't.

"What did you say to her?"

"Why do you wanna know?" she said.

"What did you say!"

The woman took a step back from the man. She

didn't like the look on his face. It reminded her of the way her father looked at her when she was a child, just before she felt the sting from the back of his hand.

"Geez, calm down," she said. "It was no big deal. She was just concerned about me and wanted to know what happened."

"You said what we went over and nothing more?"

"Yeah, just like you said."

"What did she say?"

"She gave me one of her cards," she said. "And she told me to stop by her office. But that was before the guy came out of the room and things got crazy."

"Give it to me."

"What?" she said.

"The card."

"Why?"

Sam's patience had crossed the finish line. He flashed the bills in front of her face.

"You want the money," Sam said, "give me the card."

She shrugged. "Okay."

Sam gave her the money in exchange for the card.

"Remember," he said, "there's more to come after you testify. A lot more. But keep your mouth shut and stick to the story."

The woman nodded.

"Can I ask you something?" she said. He didn't respond, so she persisted. "This guy is guilty, right? 'Cuz he just didn't look like the type of person to do all those horrible things."

Sam was halfway to his car when she finished. He turned and said, "Nice dealing with you, Trisha."

CHAPTER 35

Right outside Park City is a mountain range along a dirt–filled back road overspread with towering trees and wildflowers in all sorts of shapes and sizes. If you stand in a certain spot trees are all you see for miles and miles. Hiking was one of my favorite things to do in the whole world, especially on a day like today. The morning dew was still on many of the flowers, and the air had an aroma that was fresh and new, like the smell of rich earth when I plunged my spade into the dirt and planted my summer garden. I often thought it was what a tropical rainforest must smell like.

Lord Berkeley kept pace alongside me until he spied a butterfly, and then he was off to capture it. I reached the top of the hill and took a deep breath in, absorbing every bit of beauty the landscape offered. It was times like this when I realized just how much everyone was connected in one way or another—good and evil, young and old; we all shared a part of ourselves with the universe in which we all lived. And yet, we were all so different.

I thought about Sinnerman and what kind of a life could have driven him to his state of madness. I'd studied the profiles of other killers before him, but I never grasped what must have gone through their minds the second they killed for the first time and took their first life. A fascination with murder wasn't the only thing that plagued me. The more I studied the lifestyle, the more I came across the same thing—their troubled childhoods. It wasn't always the case, but in many instances it was, and I wondered what would have become of them had they been raised in an environment different than their own, one where they were engulfed in love. Would it have changed them from the beasts they'd later become?

I didn't know what I would do when I faced him one day. The hatred I had burned so deep within me all I could think about was seeing him dead. I pictured it in my mind over and over again. I wondered if I would be able to hold back if I ever had the chance to put an end to his wasted life. Would I take it or would I let him go? The question haunted me, following me around like an itch I constantly needed to scratch.

Halfway back to my car, I heard a sound. A twig snapped and then another. Lord Berkeley's head shot up, and he backed up to me until his body touched the front of my pant leg. He gnashed his teeth and sounded off a series of warnings, but the wooded area had gone quiet around us.

"Come on, Boo," I said. "It's okay."

He looked up at me, canvassed the woods and then gave me a look to indicate we were clear for takeoff. We made it back to my car and I opened the passenger-side door. Lord Berkeley hopped in. I then circled around to the trunk and popped it open. I tucked the bag of pinecones I'd collected to the side and then pushed the lid down.

I grabbed the door handle and heard someone approach from behind. I turned just in time to see a needle plunging toward my neck. I swerved and felt it brush the side of my face when it forced its way by me, but it didn't connect. The man who held it was dressed in a black hooded sweatshirt which he had up over his head. The tassels were tied in a bow under his chin. A blue ball cap peeked out under the hood, and his eyes were shielded by glasses that made him look like an oversized wasp. It didn't matter how many precautions he took to conceal his identity. I knew who he was.

Out of the corner of my eye, I saw Lord Berkeley inside the car trying to scratch his way through the window. I planted both feet into the soil beneath me, regained my footing and aimed my left foot straight for the groin. Upon impact the needle shot out of his gloved hand into the air and twirled around in circles before it stuck to a branch on the tree; the fluid remained inside of it. I ran to my car, whipped the door open and went for my gun. He sprinted after me, but once he saw what I held in my hand, he turned and made a mad dash for the nearest thicket of trees. I fired off a shot, and his squeal echoed around me. His hand gripped his shoulder—he'd been hit. It wasn't where I intended to get him, but at least it connected, and now the hunter had become the hunted. I was the predator, and he was my prey.

I fired off another shot, but by now he'd hidden himself well within the trees. I ran toward the path Sinnerman had hobbled across, and then stopped when I heard two more shots go off. Two other men stepped forward out of the trees. The heavy set one nodded at the thin one, and the thin one disappeared. The other guy walked toward me. I crouched down behind a tree and aimed.

"I'd stop right there if you don't want a bullet between your eyes," I said.

"Sloane, are you all right?"

"Who are you?" I said. "And how do you know my name?"

He stepped forward.

"I said stop! I'm in no mood to screw around, so don't test me."

He halted but was close enough for me now to get a

good look at him. His face was familiar, and I'd seen him months before on another case I'd worked on—he was the man in black.

"Why are you here?" I said.

"Giovanni sent us."

"Are you two the ones he's had watching out for me this whole time?"

He nodded.

"If you're here to help, can you put the gun down?" I said.

He shook his head and said, "It's for your protection."

I nodded at my 9mm and said, "I can take care of myself."

He shrugged but didn't lower his gun. It wasn't aimed at me either; it just rested by his side.

"Have you been here the whole time?" I said.

He nodded.

"How's that possible? I never knew you were there."

"Boss said not to get too close. You weren't ever supposed to see us."

"I've seen you before, six months ago," I said.

He nodded.

"Yeah, I remember."

"And I remember trying to get you to tell me your name, but you wouldn't," I said.

"It was better not to at the time," he said. "Lucio."

"What?" I said.

"That's my name. Sorry."

"For what?" I said.

"How long it took us to get to you."

"Where were you anyway?"

He walked closer to me, and I noticed his cheeks were flushed with color.

"I drank, ah, a lot of water when we got here. We was trying to keep up with you, and I wasn't doing so good, so I drank a few waters and then went over to the bushes to—"

"That's okay," I said. "I get it, no need to explain any further."

He shook his head.

"Not to you maybe, but we still have to tell the boss, and he ain't gonna be happy."

"What about the other guy?" I said. "Where was he?"

"He was supposed to keep a look out, but he got distracted by a deer. I know, sounds stupid, huh? But we don't see stuff like that where we're from."

"To be honest, I didn't know anyone was still assigned to me," I said. "Not with that guy in custody and everything."

The wrong guy.

"Boss had some doubt. Said you didn't think it was him and to stay with you until he said otherwise."

"So what else do you guys do when you're not coming to my rescue?" I said.

A smile formed on Lucio's lips, and he winked at me.

"Nice try, lady." He wagged his finger at me. "For a smart girl, I can't believe you haven't figured it out yet. You expect me to believe you don't know?"

A figure appeared from the side of a huge boulder. We raised our guns in synchronized motion.

Lucio shouted, "Sal, that you?"

"It's me," the guy said.

Lucio turned to me. "It's okay, he's one of us." He gave Sal a stern look and said,

"Well?"

Sal shrugged but wouldn't look him in the eye.

"Can't find him. I looked everywhere. No blood, nothin'. It's like the guy was never here."

"Boss won't be happy 'bout this," he said.

"I'll talk to him," I said.

Sal and Lucio looked at each other and laughed. Lucio said, "Lady, you got a lot to learn."

I didn't say a word. So did they.

CHAPTER 36

Sam Reids hunched over the stove in his kitchen and nursed his wound. The bullet from Sloane's gun nicked him in the shoulder, and it stung like he'd doused it in alcohol and held it there. Going to the hospital was out of the question—he'd have to extract the bullet himself.

He took a long swig of whiskey, and another, and then poured some of it on the afflicted area. It was now or never. With his sterilized knife in hand, Sam stabbed at the gaping hole. The impact of the knife on his exposed flesh was more than he could stand, and he squealed like a pig headed for the slaughter. He jerked from one side to the other and wished he could knock himself unconscious rather than endure the pain a second more.

Sam tried to set aside the constant throb that pounded like the beat of a heart and inched the knife deeper until he reached the place where the bullet had lodged. He dug around until he had a firm grip and then harvested it from its position inside his body. He grabbed it with his free hand and heaved it across the room. It smacked hard against the wall and fell in silence to the carpet below. Sam dipped the blade of his knife into the open flame on his gas stove and then, when it was hot enough, he pressed it against his flesh. The smell permeated the room, and it looked like his flesh had melted, but after a moment, the wound seared shut and he tossed the knife into the sink.

Sam didn't want to admit his plan had turned out to be such a grandiose failure or that Sloane was more prepared than he anticipated. She was alone, vulnerable, and in the perfect position for him to strike, and yet he'd failed. He thought it would be easier to catch her—he was sure she would struggle, but to fight back like she did without hesitation, purely on instinct, was a shock to him. Sloane was strong and resilient. To catch her would require serious thought.

He hadn't planned on the two goons who showed up either. The bait he set with the fake Sinnerman in custody had all been for naught. Why hadn't her protection been called off like he thought would happen—didn't they think they had their killer? It didn't make sense. She should have been in his possession now, locked up in a room in his basement that he'd prepared just for her, his most prized possession. But his plan had failed, and he wondered how long it would take for it all to unravel.

Now there were loose ends to take care of, and he cringed at the thought of it. Sam wanted nothing more than to make Sloane pay. He'd make them all pay.

CHAPTER 37

I sat on a sofa in a room the size of my entire house that was embellished in warm shades of burgundy, brown, and gold. Every wall was adorned with at least one piece of art, many were works by famous artists, but unlike so many replicas I'd seen in other homes, I had no doubt they were originals.

In another room a group of men were involved in a conversation of some kind. From what I could hear, it was Giovanni, Sal, and Lucio. Giovanni tried to muffle his voice and keep a sense of composure, but his tone was tense, his words—sharp. He reprimanded them for letting me out of their sight because Sinnerman was still out there somewhere and what that reality meant for me, and what that would mean for them if anything happened to me because of it. His voice conveyed genuine concern, and I wasn't sure how I felt about that. A minute later, the only sound I heard was the persistent twitch of the clock that hung on the wall in front of me. The front door closed, and Giovanni joined me in the living room.

"I know it doesn't change things," I said, "but they did try to protect me."

He sat down next to me and remitted a cup of tea.

"I didn't mean for you to hear our conversation."

"For whatever reason, lately I've felt like the girl in school who gets all the boys in trouble. I didn't know I was still being shadowed by your men, or I never would have gone up there in the first place and put them through all that. I'm sure they drained themselves just to keep up. There's no way they could have been expected to—"

He placed his hand on my leg, which stopped me midsentence. Why did I lose all concentration every single time he got anywhere near any part of my body? It bugged me.

"I don't want anything to happen to you, Sloane," he said.

His sentiment was too much, too soon, and I wished for an eject button on the side of the chair to hurl me toward the sky before I felt any more out of my element than I already did. Giovanni just sat there and stared into my eyes with such tenacity—the confidence I usually had, but for right now, for whatever reason, I lacked. Instead, I pointed at one of the paintings on the wall and said, "Which one is your favorite? They're all so different from each other." Lame.

"All of them. I have a deep appreciation for art, which I attribute to the fact that I cannot draw to save my life. And I've found that when I'm unable to do something, I either learn how to, or in this case, I gain a much deeper respect for it."

"Books do the same thing to me," I said. "I never did any good in English class, and the grades I received on my essays were even worse. It's easier for me to pick up a book and get swept away with how the words are articulated on the page. It's a feeling I can't describe. Reading brings me so much happiness. I become so engrossed in the story, I forget everything going on around me."

"We have a great deal in common."

"I think so too," I said.

"We should talk about what happened to you today."

I sat back, crossed my legs, and took a sip of my tea.

"It was him," I said. "Sinnerman."

His face turned from playful and soft to grim in an instant.

"You're sure?"

I nodded.

"He approached me from behind with a needle, and we already know he sedates his victims when he takes them," I said. "It's his M-O."

There was a knock at the door. He looked at me and said, "Will you excuse me for a moment?"

A minute later Giovanni's brother and the chief entered the room. The chief looked like he'd had about twenty cups of coffee and all the added sugar he could stand.

"Sloane, are you all right?" the chief said.

I nodded.

"I'm doing fine."

I felt like I'd been shaken and stirred, but I didn't want everyone else to know. Just being in the presence of the man I'd hunted for the last few years roused all kinds of emotions inside me. I was so close, and now all I could think of was whether I'd get another chance or if I'd blown it all together.

"You got something for me?" Agent Luciana said.

I nodded and rose from the chair and walked over to a small round table at the corner of the room. I reached into the drawer and pulled out the needle Lucio had freed from its home on high.

"I didn't have any plastic with me," I said. "So the only thing I could do was fold it in a napkin I had in my car."

Agent Luciana took it and thanked me. It was *all business, all the time* with him.

"I doubt you'll get any prints off it; he was wearing gloves," I said.

He nodded.

"Just what in the hell is this guy after anyway?" Agent Luciana said.

"Isn't it obvious?" I said. "Me."

The chief and Agent Luciana exchanged looks and then sat down on the sofa. I sat across from them. Giovanni stood in the corner of the room, leaned up against the wall with his arms crossed.

"Go on," the chief said.

"This is the way I see it—for whatever reason, Sinnerman wanted everyone to believe he'd been caught. He framed a guy for the murders, planted evidence in the guy's car, and had every last detail organized. It was a well-choreographed operation. And he was so good at it, you all believed you'd caught the killer, and who knows, maybe you still believe it. All I know is he went through a lot of effort to pull this off so everyone would stop looking for him. And when he thought he'd succeeded, the first thing he did was to come after me."

"What does he want with you though?" the chief said. "All his other women have been random. Why single you out—I mean I get there's a sister connection, but…"

I shrugged.

"Maybe because I called him out. Who knows? No other woman has been bold enough. But to put all this together just so he could get his grips on me…"

"I've seen this type of thing before," Agent Luciana said. "Not in this exact way, but I believe he's become obsessed with you, and I'd be willing to bet there's no avenue he won't consider in order to get what he wants. There's a term for his behavior: erotomania."

"Eroto what?" I said.

"It's when a person suffers with a form of delusion where they believe the other person is in love with them. They live in some type of fantasy until they feel betrayed, at which point, they can become violent. I believe he's been stalking you for some time."

"Why me?" I said.

Giovanni walked over next to me and sat down.

"Because of who you are," he said. "You're gutsy; you let him know you were coming after him. You told me yourself that you believe this guy gets his kicks from a challenge, and I've never known a better one than you."

"If he wants me, he can come and get me," I said. "I have another bullet for him, and this time it will be aimed straight at his chest."

CHAPTER 38

Three hours later I stepped out of my car and into a local joint known for being the place to go if you wanted to score, and by score, I didn't mean a one-night stand. My attire for the evening was black. A fitted black t-shirt with shredded holes on both sides, faded jeans, and dark makeup, and I'd gone so heavy on the eyeliner I could have attracted a male raccoon. I felt like a prostitute, and I imagined I looked the part as well.

After I'd sorted the morning's events around in my head, I realized there was one person I needed to talk to who was the best chance I had to find Sinnerman—Trisha. She'd fingered the guy in custody fast—too fast. And then there was the matter of her bloody nose. For a girl who claimed to live where she did, the way she dressed told me otherwise.

Behind the counter at the bar was a giant of a teenager with bluish hair accented with black tips on the ends. It was shaped into perfect spikes on top of his squarish head. The spikes reminded me of the points on a stegosaurus, and they were so stiff, I wanted to ask him what kind of hairspray he used for future reference. He eyed me with a look of disdain.

"You gonna order lady, or what?"

I shook my head.

"Nobody comes in here and doesn't get a drink or something, okay?"

"Fine. I'll take the *or something*," I said.

His forehead creased into several lines that spanned the length of his head.

"What'll it be?"

For the sake of appearances, I knew I needed to order before he became unnerved enough to tip everyone off to the imposter lurking about the place. The last thing I needed was the fine patrons of the seedy establishment to clear out like a bomb had just gone off.

"You got any absinthe?"

He nodded.

"One shot," I said.

"A shot of it?"

"You heard me," I said.

He shook his head and relayed the order to the lanky woman who stood behind him. Her extra-small tank top hung off her body like a piece of torn fabric in the wind. While she poured my drink, my favorite girl-who-cried-wolf meandered through the door. She looked disheveled, just like the first time we met, except this time there was one difference: she fondled a wad of cash in her right hand. She didn't notice me, and that was fine. It gave me a chance to observe her. And the first thing she did was to head straight for a back room. I waited and as I did so, I weighed my options about whether or not to take the shot in front of me. I took it.

"Another?" the bartender said when I'd finished.

I shot him a wink and edged off the barstool.

"I'd like something a bit stronger," I said, and tilted my head toward the door Trisha just went through.

"Ahh," he said. "I see."

I didn't, but I was about to. I made my way through the crowd and stood a couple feet from where Trisha had just entered. It didn't take long for her to reemerge, and by the smile smeared across her face, it looked like she'd gotten what she wanted. She made her way to the entrance and walked out of the bar without a word to anyone. I followed.

When I got outside Trisha was about twenty paces in front of me.

"Where you headed?" I said.

Trisha curved her body around. She had a stunned look on her face, and once she got over her initial shock, she walked in my direction.

"Oh, it's you. What are you doing here?"

"I came to ask you a question," I said.

"Which is?"

"I want to know why an innocent man is in custody."

Her eyes widened, and she placed her hand over her heart.

"What are you talking about?"

"Oh come on—you know. And I've been thinking, what could motivate a person enough to send an innocent man to trial?"

She looked at the ground.

"Don't want to say it out loud?" I said. "Fine, allow me. Drugs."

"I don't do drugs."

"Turn out your pockets," I said. "Prove it."

"You don't have the right to tell me to do anything," she said. She spread both hands out to the side like she was trying to push air away from her and said, "I'm outta here."

Trisha steadied herself and looked like she was about to make tracks, but she didn't get far before Sal and Lucio circumvented her escape. Each grabbed one of her arms and in simultaneous motion yanked her back toward the car.

"What—where you taking—? Get your hands off me!"

Once they reached the car, Lucio threw her into the back seat. Sal fastened a zip tie around her wrists and said, "Make a sound lady, and I tape your mouth shut."

"You can't do this to me!"

I reached into Trisha's jacket pocket and jerked out a bag of white powder and stuffed it into the side of the seat. Trisha shrieked like she was in the throes of severe labor pains.

"Oh zip it," I said. "This stuff is the reason why you're in this mess. That and plain stupidity."

"Give it back, it's mine. Bought and paid for. You've no right to—"

Sal had taken all he could stand. He yanked off a piece of sticky white tape and smacked it across her lips.

"Let me know when you calm down so we can communicate with each other," I said, "or the tape stays on and your hands remain tied."

It took about four minutes for her to give me a look to indicate she was throwing out the white flag.

"I'm going to ask you some questions," I said, "and I don't want to hear any bullshit, got it? If you lie to me, I'll know."

She nodded, and I removed the tape from her lips.

"Why did you lie about what happened to you?" I said.

She thought about it and then said, "I didn't."

I waved the tape out in front of me.

"Okay, okay," she said. "I needed the money."

I shook my head. "Not good enough. Start from the

beginning."

She buried her head in her hands and was silent. I waited.

"So I'm in the bar one night—"

"Which bar?"

"The one we were just at."

"Go on," I said.

"And this guy comes up to me and says do I wanna make some extra cash. I ask him how much extra cash he was talkin' about and he said it depended."

"On what?"

"He had a couple jobs for me to do, and each time I did what he asked, I'd get more money."

"What did he look like?"

"I've only seen him twice," she said. "Once in the bar, and once at the gas station. Both times he wore a sweatshirt and a cap on his head."

"Do you remember what the hat had on it, what color—anything?"

"It was for that one team." She thought about it for a minute. "It had a big 'C' on it."

"Was it blue with a red brim and the C was done in red stitching?"

She nodded. "Yeah, yeah, that's the one. But what I thought was really weird was he wouldn't ever take his glasses off, and both times I saw him, it was like, at night." She shrugged. "I didn't get it. Thought he was just some weirdo or something, but hey, if he wanted to offer me money, I didn't care how big of a freak the guy was."

She had no idea.

"What did he ask you to do?" I said.

"He said I needed to get all roughed up like I'd just been in a fight and then go into the police station at eleven o'clock the next day. He showed me a picture of some guy and said when I saw him, I had to tell everyone he was the man who tried to assault me."

"And the shiner?"

"He punched me."

"Who did?" I said.

"The guy who hired me. He said he had to so it looked real."

"You let the guy hit you for some pocket change to feed your drug habit? Pathetic."

She smirked at me.

"It wasn't a little bit of cash, honey. It was five large."

Sal and Lucio looked at each other but didn't utter a word.

"That's a lot of money," I said.

She laughed.

"He said if I testified, he'd pay me ten thousand. Cash."

"And you didn't care about the innocent guy who'd get locked away for the rest of his life?"

"I didn't know."

"What do you mean you didn't know?" I said.

"The guy said he was an undercover agent trying to bust the guy in the Sinnerman murders. He said they knew it was him, that they just needed a witness to make sure the guy went to prison. The way I saw it, I was doing every chick in this town a favor."

"Except that the guy who paid you was the real Sinnerman," I said, "and the one locked away is just some scared kid who hasn't hurt anyone in his life."

"You're not serious?" she said. "That can't be."

I looked her straight in the eye. "It is. And do you want to know who he just came after? Me." I said. "He attacked *me*."

Trisha didn't speak much for the rest of the drive, and I couldn't tell whether she was scared or full of regret or both. I assumed it was both. She looked out her window into the black of night and pretended to sleep, but she didn't fool me. I was too repulsed by her to continue this on my own. I'd hand her over to Coop when I got to the station, and he could take it from there. I didn't know what to believe about the story she told. She seemed to express genuine remorse, but I'd dealt with plenty of druggies before and was seasoned in the way they could make a person believe the blue sky was red when they needed to.

We parked, and Sal and Lucio got out. Lucio walked with me, and Sal tended to our drug addict. When I reached the station door, I heard a sound behind me, like a pop. I turned. Blood streamed from the middle of Trisha's forehead, and then another pop echoed in the distance and Sal collapsed to the ground, blood gushing from his chest. I tried to run toward them, but Lucio shielded me with his body and thrust me into the doors of the station. Rose looked at me like I was as mad as a hatter, and out of the corner of my eye, I saw Coop rush to my side.

"What's going on out there?" he said.

"Two people have been shot," I yelled. "Do something!"

CHAPTER 39

By the time Coop and the rest of the guys swarmed around Trisha and Sal, it was too late—they were both dead, and the hunt was on to find the location from which the shots had been fired. Agent Luciana arrived several minutes later and pushed his way past the reporters that had pullulated around the place. He headed straight for me, grabbing the edge of my sweater, and walking me over to the corner of the room.

"Can we talk?" he said.

I nodded. He looked over at Lucio and said, "Wait here." Lucio reclined into an office chair and folded his arms and tilted his head back toward the wall like he was ready for his evening nap. I couldn't figure out how he remained so calm. My body felt like an electric current flowed through it.

Agent Luciana raised his hand and gestured down the hall, and we walked into an unoccupied room. He closed the door and then rested the weight of his body against the back of it. With both hands, he pressed hard into the sides of his face and then rested them there until he decided to speak.

"This is a disaster," he said. "Did you at least get her to talk before she died?"

I nodded and filled him in on the details.

When I finished, he said, "This guy has a much deeper agenda than I thought."

"Have you released the kid in custody yet?"

"Not yet, we were waiting."

"For what—a sign or something that you had the wrong guy? Because if you are, this is it."

"Your attitude doesn't help," he said.

"You need to find him—fast."

"And how do you suggest I go about it? This guy's a ghost—an expert at evading everyone."

"Every killer has a weakness."

"And what might his be?" he said.

I took a deep breath and looked him in the eye.

"We both know the answer to that. You're looking at her."

*****

"You look like you're about to fall asleep on that chair."

I looked up at a smiling Giovanni who hovered over me.

"Just got caught up in my thoughts," I said. "My mind never really shuts off. I am kinda tired though."

After the attempt on my life and the assassinations at the station, Giovanni insisted I stay at his house, and his brother agreed. It was the safest place I could be, and since there were cameras all over and men wandering around like a bunch of whatchamacallits, I believed him.

"Let me show you the room you'll be staying in," he said.

I lifted my arms into the air, stretched them out to both sides, and yawned.

"It's just for tonight."

Giovanni gave me a look that made me feel like I wouldn't be going home anytime soon, and then he turned and walked down the hall. I followed. At the midway point, he opened a door and stepped inside.

"I hope this works for you," he said.

I looked around. In all my life I'd never stayed in a room so lavish. It mirrored the décor in the living room except in the center of the room, instead of a sofa and chairs, was an enormous four poster bed fit for a queen, and I had one thing on my mind—sleep.

*****

When I opened my eyes the next morning Maddie was sitting on a chair diagonal from the bed. I sat up and leaned my head back against the headboard.

"You slept long enough," she said. "I've been worried about you since Wade told me what happened to you in the woods. And thanks for calling by the way."

I'd wanted to tell her everything before the chief did, but it had all happened so fast.

"I'm sorry. Have you been here awhile?"

"Long enough to hear you chatter in your sleep."

"I don't chatter."

She rolled her eyes.

"I just listened to fifteen minutes of non-stop talking."

"About what?"

"It was hard to make out," she said. "You blabbed on and on, and you were out of breath, like you were running away from something—or someone."

I had a good idea of who the someone was.

"How'd you know I was here?"

"I have my ways, and on that subject," she thumbed in the direction of the doorway, "what a little hottie he is."

"Who—Giovanni?"

"Who else? Surprised to see you slept in a different room though."

"Maddie!"

She bobbed her shoulders up and down.

"What—you know me. I would have tapped that once, if not twice, if I was in your position. I'm just sayin'."

"It's not like he's taken."

"Girl, please. The man's talked about you nonstop since I got here. So do you like him, or what?"

"Too much is going on right now for me to even consider it."

Maddie walked over and sat down next to me on the edge of the bed. "Make time for him," she said. "Don't let something that delicious get away."

"I see what you're doing."

"Which is?" she said.

"You know I can't let anything distract me right now, not until—"

Giovanni tapped on the door a few times and then came in.

"Would you ladies care for some breakfast?" he said.

"You bet," Maddie said.

He looked in my direction.

"Sloane?"

"I don't want you to put yourself out," I said.

He made a face that reminded me of a disgruntled employee, so I tried again.

"I'm starved," I said. "Thank you."

He smiled and said, "It will be ready in ten," and then he turned and shut the door behind him.

Once he left, Maddie prodded me in the arm with two of her fingers.

"What was that for?" I said.

"If you don't stop acting so passive the guy is going

to think you'd rather get with some over-the-hill senior citizen than with him."

"Oh stop it," I said. "He understands. Have you examined the bodies from last night?"

She nodded and said, "Strange, don't you think?"

"Because he used a gun?" I said.

"Yeah."

"He's angry," I said. "I shot him and ruined his plans. It forced him to clean up the mess he made, which started with Trisha. He wanted to kill her before she got the chance to talk, but he was too late."

"And the other guy?"

"Sal? Wrong place, wrong time, maybe."

"So why not you? He must have had a clear shot at some point, but he didn't even try for you."

"It's like he skipped over me on purpose. Think about it, Maddie. He set this whole scheme up, framed someone for murder, and paid someone to help him do it. There has to be a driving force behind it—he wants something."

"Not something—someone," she said. "You."

"And a guy like him won't stop until he gets what he wants."

CHAPTER 40

After breakfast, Maddie left, and I showered and got ready—for what, I didn't know. I was in the middle of towel-drying my hair when a sound emanated from my phone.

"How are you?" I said.

"Why?" Nick said. "It's not like you care."

"Of course I do."

"Why?"

"Where are you?" I said.

"Doesn't matter."

"Are you coming back?"

"Would it make a difference if I did?"

"I still care about you," I said.

He laughed into the phone.

"Right. You care. From what I hear, you have someone else to look out for you now. I have to say, I knew it would happen, but not this fast."

"It's not what you think," I said.

"Isn't it? You slept at his house last night."

Damn Coop, and damn his big mouth. I was sure he was the one who let that information slip out.

"Nick, why did you call me?" I said.

"It was a mistake."

And the line went dead.

I wrapped my bath towel around me and fell back on the bed and closed my eyes. I tried to muster up some tears, but they didn't come, and I didn't know why. After all, we'd had a long relationship and I'd loved him—hadn't I? I thought back to any memories I had where I remembered shedding tears of any kind. I could count them on one and a half hands. I didn't lack feeling or emotion, just the ability to express my feelings like most other people. My life felt more in control this way. I'd never understood how most women cried as easily as the rain falling from a wispy cloud on a dark and dreary day. How was it possible?

It was moments like these when I was all alone in a room with nothing but my thoughts to keep me company that I needed to be careful. I had to watch the bottle I'd set out to sea to make sure it didn't come loose or worse—pop off and spray my emotions in the air for all the world to see.

During our relationship, Nick had prompted me to see a counselor. But all I could think about was how it would feel to be shrink-wrapped by some head case in a stuffy office painted in depressed shades of beige and decorated with knock-off leather office furniture that squeaked every time my butt shifted a couple of inches. He said I needed to go in order to get past my sister. But there was no getting past Gabrielle; for me, there was but one option—closure. And no shrink could provide it. That was something I had to do for myself.

"Where are you off to today then?"

The sound of Giovanni's voice entering the room thrust me back into the world again. I pulled my towel until it was tight and twisted the corner into a thick point and shoved it into my cleavage and sat up.

"I need to get Boo," I said. "He's my—"

"Westie, yes I know."

"I'm sure he's confused about why he was left all alone last night."

"That might not be entirely true," he said.

Giovanni pressed a button on the wall box in my room. A few seconds later, Lord Berkeley bounded into my room and hopped up on the bed with me. His tail wagged like a jogger on a treadmill at full speed. I grabbed the snowy ball of fur and held him tight to me. Behind him a woman entered the room. I hadn't seen her in some time, and I wished more than ever I had taken the time to get dressed when I had the chance.

"It's good to see you," she said.

"And you, Daniela. I didn't know you lived here."

She shook her head.

"I'm just in town to pester my dear brother," she said with a wink in his direction, "but I can see he's found plenty of other things to occupy his time." She looked at Giovanni. "Sloane will be staying for dinner, right?"

"It's up to her."

She looked at me with a gleam of hope.

"You must," she said. "We need to catch up."

I'd never known her to be so friendly, but then again, the last time we met had been under different circumstances. She'd been the recipient of physical abuse, but he was now six feet under.

"Sure," I said. "I'd love to."

"Well, see you both later then. I've got some shopping to do."

Daniela turned and darted out the door.

"What now?" Giovanni said.

I had no idea. I looked at Giovanni and then to Lord Berkeley who was asleep in my lap. In that moment, everything of importance was right there with me in my room.

*****

It didn't take much for Giovanni to convince me to make my stay an extended one. I thought I'd want to cry out in protest, but when he made the offer, I accepted without much hesitation.

My cell phone rang again, and this time I was dressed and ready. The name on the screen said The Pretty Pen.

"Hi, Robert," I said.

"Sorry it took so long to get back to you," he said. "I have some news, but I'm afraid it will be of little use to you."

"I'll take whatever you can give me."

"The paper you gave me isn't manufactured anymore, and it hasn't been for some time."

"How long has it been discontinued—do you know?" I said.

"Twenty years, maybe more."

I couldn't believe it.

"Do you have any idea what it was used for?" I said.

"It wasn't very popular, and since it was such a long time ago, none of my distributors have any records showing who they sold it to."

"So how did you know it hasn't been made for so long?" I said.

"I scanned the paper and sent it to several companies I do business with. One of them is a specialty store that deals with art schools for the most part. The manager there had worked for the company for over thirty years and had a vague memory that they stocked that type of paper back in the day."

"Thanks for the call; you've helped me a lot more than you realize," I said.

I pressed the end button on my phone and went through the house until I found Giovanni. He was the center of attention in a huddle of men, all dressed in varied shades of black. When I approached I felt like I'd interrupted what appeared to be a serious conversation. I tried to backtrack out of the room, but Giovanni saw me—it was too late.

"Sloane," he said, "come in."

He flicked his right hand twice and the men around him dispersed, and in a few seconds it was like they were never there. A thick cloud of smoke permeated the air in the room. Cigars.

"What is it?" Giovanni said.

"It's nothing. Sorry to barge in on you."

"We're finished, and you're never a bother."

"Are you available for a little excursion?" I said.

"With you—always."

CHAPTER 41

Park City offered much more than some of the world's most exclusive ski resorts. Summer brought on the arts festival, and all the galleries in town sparked to life. In addition to various shows and exhibits, the town was also home to a variety of art schools, including the one that Giovanni and I had just parked in front of.

The Park City Institute of the Arts was a school dedicated to producing the next mini-Michelangelos. It was housed in a brick building and looked like it was erected around the same time the rest of the town was. When I exited the car, I looked up to the center window on the second floor and could have sworn I saw someone peek out of it. It was then I realized I'd seen far too many episodes of *Ghost Hunters*.

The school had vacated for the summer, and the parking lot was empty except for a single car parked next to ours. The front door had been propped open about the length of my foot and was secured in place with a brown cinder block. Giovanni pulled the door all the way back, and we walked in.

I cupped my hands around the outside of my mouth and shouted, "Hello?"

"Back here," a female voice said.

I followed the sound into an office, where an older woman was hunched over a pile of supplies. When she saw me, she rubbed both of her hands together and brushed them off on her tweed pants and stood.

"Forgive the mess," she said, "summer is just about the only time I get to organize this place."

"I understand."

"What can I do for you two? Do you have children you'd like to enroll?"

Giovanni's eyes darted to me and softened, and a huge grin covered his face.

"Oh no," I said. "We aren't, well, what I mean to say is, we don't have any—"

"Children together," Giovanni said.

I looked at him and mouthed the words thank you. My face burned like it was on fire.

"No children?" the woman said.

Giovanni smiled at me, winked, and said, "Not yet."

His comment startled me, and I wondered if it was his idea of a joke, but there was something about the way he said it that didn't sound like one at all. He just continued to smile, and I realized he'd said it to get a rise out of me. He'd succeeded.

"Have you worked here long?" I said to the woman.

"Oh, about thirty years or so; why do you ask?"

"I wondered if you could take a look at a piece of paper and tell me if you recognize it."

She held her hand out.

"Sure."

"Before I show it to you though, I need you to understand the contents are personal in nature, and you can't talk about what you read with anyone," I said.

She giggled like a child in grade school.

"These days there aren't too many people for me to talk to, hun, but if it makes you feel any better, you have my promise; I won't breathe a word."

Her tiny, curious eyes reminded me of my grandmother, and I believed what she said was true. I unzipped my bag and took out the pink parchment and showed it to her. She turned it around in her hand without much heed to the words written on the front.

The woman looked at Giovanni and then aimed her finger at a box in the corner.

"Would you mind getting my glasses?"

Giovanni grabbed them and opened them up for her. She put them on.

"Much better," she said. She rubbed the parchment in between her fingers and then said, "I haven't seen paper like this for ages."

"Do you recognize it?"

"It looks like its intended use was for artists so you're on the right track there, but we've never used this at our school. Not as long as I've been here."

Her words gripped me like a noose around my neck. This was the oldest art school in town. Maybe my hunch had steered me in the wrong direction.

"Well," I said, taking the paper back from her, "it was worth a try. It was nice to meet you. Thanks for your time."

"You bet, dear."

We headed for the door, but before we exited, I turned to ask one final question.

"I know it's a long shot, but are there any other schools around here from a couple decades ago?"

She took some time to think about it and then said, "Well, yes. There is one. But it's been closed for many years."

"Can you tell me where it is?"

"Right behind the library. It's an old, yellow building. Hasn't been used for much of anything since it shut down."

"Do you know the name of the owner or why it closed?" I said.

She laughed. "You're really testing my memory today. Seems like the woman's name was Laurel or

Lauren if I remember right. And as to why it closed, well, all I can tell you is the rumor back then was that the owner up and left town with her new beau."

"She was married at the time?"

The woman nodded.

"Had a child too. Can't tell you whether the rumor was true or not, but I do know this—she never came back."

*****

Ten minutes later Giovanni and I stood in front of an old wood house, and one thing was clear—it hadn't been occupied for some time. A white picket fence in desperate need of a splash of color surrounded the perimeter of the property. A couple of the double-pane windows had holes in the glass about the size of a golf ball, and the front walk was overrun with weeds. From a distance, I could see the door knob had been broken off and was sealed shut by a couple rusty nails that had been drilled into the frame.

I turned to Giovanni. "Are you up to this, because I'd understand if you wanted to wait in the car."

His response was swift. He walked in front of me and squared off with the front door. After he gripped it with his fingers and pulled back a few times, he said, "The door is sealed shut. Let's try this another way."

The first two windows Giovanni yanked on wouldn't

budge, so we went around to the back of the house—
again to no avail. The windows were sealed so tightly it
was like they'd become one with the walls. Giovanni
grabbed a rock the size of his fist and looked at me.

"Do you object?"

"Not at all. Clearly this isn't a place of business
anymore."

I pulled my zip-up sweater from around my waist
and held it out. "Here, use this. I don't want you to cut
yourself."

At first I thought he was going to tell me what a
tough guy he was. Instead, he grabbed me and propelled
me forward, and the next thing I knew I was enveloped
in his arms, and I had no desire to disengage anytime
soon.

Several seconds later he released me, and within a
minute we were inside the decrepit building. From the
moment we entered the place, I was overcome by two
things: a sensation of sheer exhilaration and the
overwhelming smell of a dingy, stuffy, old house. I
sheathed my nose with my hand and looked around.
Papers were scattered across the floor, paintings had been
overturned, and the desk in the corner of the room had
been deprived of its three pull-out drawers.

The place had been ransacked—and I guessed on
more than one occasion. Just the sight of the destruction
filled me with sadness, and I thought about what it must

have been like back in its heyday when it was filled with the hopes and dreams of aspiring young artists who lined the halls with their work.

Giovanni reached down and scooped up a pile of papers. "The old woman was right," he said. "There was a Laurel here at one time."

He handed the stack of papers over to me. The one on top of the pile looked like an enrollment agreement for one of the students, and at the bottom of the page was a box with typed letters that said administrator and above it the signature of Laurel Reids.

I set the papers on top of a thick layer of dust that had collected on the desk and scavenged around to see what else I could find. In the next room, stacked against the wall, I noticed a row of several easels and a few wooden chairs. A few paintings remained, but they were ruined and haphazardly thrown to the floor. One rested with the painted side down. I scooped it up and turned it over, but it was too dirty to make out the picture at first. I brushed it off with the palm of my hand and then wiped my hands on my jeans. It wasn't the most sanitary thing to do, but it was my only option. The oil painting was of a girl who couldn't have been more than seven years old at the time. Her dark bangs fell loosely along her forehead and into her eyes, but not so much that I couldn't see them. She was so young, but her eyes didn't tell the story of a joyful child. They reflected something else—a sadness of some kind, and I imagined tears welled up in those enormous brown eyes of hers.

I rubbed the bottom corner of the picture with my thumb and read the signature of the artist: L. Reids.

From the other end of the room, Giovanni shouted that he'd found a cabinet of supplies.

"Come take a look at this," he said.

I made my way over to him and pulled the cabinet door back until it was all the way open. There, on the second shelf in the center of the cabinet, was a wire basket filled with white parchment paper. When I lifted the paper to get a closer look, I noticed another type of paper on the bottom of the stack. It was pink.

CHAPTER 42

"What would you like to do now?" Giovanni said.

I shrugged and looked at the pink paper I'd taken from the art school.

"I suppose we need to let your brother know about this."

He nodded.

"That would be wise."

"I'd like to have some time first before I make the call—I want to dig around a little bit on the Internet and see what I can find. I'm sure your brother wishes I wasn't involved in this, but I am, and this is the only way I can stay a step ahead of everyone. Otherwise, they will leave me out, I'm sure of it."

"No need to explain," he said.

Is there anything about this guy that isn't perfect?

*****

We stopped by my place so I could grab my laptop and

some clothes, and then drove back to Giovanni's for dinner.

My Internet search proved profitable, and with a few keywords I was able to find some additional information on Laurel Reids. Ms. Reids was the wife of a wealthy oil tycoon by the name of Decklan Reids, until she bailed on their relationship. She left behind not only a thriving art institute, but her husband and son, and just like the old woman had said earlier, I found no record that Ms. Reids had ever returned. I wondered why.

From what I could tell, Decklan Reids stayed in the area and still lived in the same house in Park Meadows. I jotted down the address. I wasn't sure where all of this would lead, but something stirred inside me that had been unmoved since Gabrielle's death, and I felt my whole body burn at the prospect of achieving my goal: catching Sinnerman.

After an unforgettable dinner with Giovanni and his sister which included Lord Berkeley eating out of a marble dog bowl that seemed to be purchased just for the occasion, I set out to see whether Decklan Reids still occupied the house on 3873 Pinedale Street. A part of me wanted to go it alone. I did my best PI work in solitary, but I knew even Giovanni couldn't grant me that kind of leniency.

*****

The lights were on when we arrived at Decklan Reids' house. We approached the front door and knocked. A thin woman with short, white, curly hair in a crisp sundress with an apron over the top opened the door.

"Can I help you?"

"Is this the home of Decklan Reids?" I said.

"It is."

"I hoped I could speak with him," I said. "Is he here?"

She wiped her hands on her apron and said, "Just a moment. Let me see if he is available."

She left us at the doorway, and a minute later, a man arrived at the door. He was taller than most men I'd met, with grey hair and the body of a runner. He glanced at me and then Giovanni but did not speak—he just stood there, waiting for one of us to say something first. So I did.

"Mr. Reids, I hoped I could speak to you for a moment."

"About?"

"Can we come in? I'd rather discuss it inside if you don't mind," I said.

"I don't even know who you are."

I brandished my card and gave it to him.

He held it about four inches away from his face and squashed his eyes together while he gazed at it.

"What are you investigating?"

Giovanni and I exchanged glances. I didn't want to

blurt out information about my investigation into the Sinnerman murders, but I had to compel him enough to let me through the front door.

"I'm looking for Laurel Reids. I believe she was your wife," I said.

"Ex-wife."

"I'm sorry, yes."

"That was a long time ago. And I can't see what use I would be. Why?"

"One of her art students is trying to reach her," I said.

Oh what a tangled web we weave.

"After so long?"

I nodded.

"Any help you can give us would be appreciated."

He pondered it for a bit and then backed away a few steps.

"Come in."

We followed him through the parlor and into the living room. It was decorated in rich tones of navy blue and tan with deep brown accents. My first impression screamed *bachelor.* The furniture was rustic and reminded me of something I would see in a log cabin. In the center of the room a knotty log hearth was placed over the fireplace, and above it on the wall was the biggest moose head I'd ever seen in my life.

Decklan beamed and said to Giovanni, "Shot that one myself." Giovanni didn't seem the least bit interested, but he nodded and smiled.

"Do you hunt often?" I said.

"Every chance I get. Been on every continent and hunted everything from elephants to javelinas. Care to see my trophy room?"

I was certain Giovanni lacked interest in a room full of stuffed dead animals, but he also seemed aware of the fact that I would seize any opportunity to snoop, so he nodded a reluctant yes.

"And you?" Decklan said, and turned to me.

"I'll wait here, if you don't mind."

Decklan shrugged his shoulders.

"Suit yourself."

Once they were out of sight, I made my move. Ever since we'd arrived I had my eye on a room down the hall. While we stood in the living room and chatted, I could see the entrance of what appeared to be a boy's room, and my curiosity was piqued. With no one in sight, I booked it down the hall. I passed a bathroom on the left which I made note of; it could serve me well if Giovanni and Decklan decided to hike back up the stairs early, although I was certain Giovanni would keep him at bay. I knew he wouldn't hesitate to flex his persuasive muscle if needed.

The door at the end of the hall was slightly ajar when I reached it. I nudged it with my arm just enough that I could slide in and out with ease. Once inside, I glanced around. The blue and green plaid twin comforter had been made up to perfection, and it matched the tab-topped curtains that hung over the two oversized windows in the room. There was a single wood dresser with black metal circular knobs, two on each drawer. The walls were sparse with little adornment, but there were holes to indicate things had been hung on them at some point in the past. Some of the holes were spaced apart in a square pattern, the exact size of a poster; it made me curious.

On top of the dresser there were several framed photos of a child at various stages of life. In one, he looked to be about four. He held up a giant fish attached to a long rod. A much younger Decklan stood next to him with the proud parent smile plastered across his face. And there had been a third person in the photo, but it had been ripped, and all that remained was a hand from the person on the boy's arm. The boy's eyes were fixed on the fish with an innate fascination, but he didn't smile like his father. His face was emotionless.

In another photo, the boy was older. He posed with a deer of some kind, or maybe it was an elk. From the look of it, the animal was dead, and the boy was covered in blood. But something else stood out—the boy's hands, his left one in particular. In the photo at four years of age, his hands were perfect. But something happened between the first photo and the second. A few of his fingers on his left hand were bent over in such a way they appeared to have been mangled, almost like he'd contracted some sort of disease that caused them to degenerate. Yet, his other hand looked just fine.

Behind the photo of the boy and the animal was an album. I grabbed it and flipped through its pages. It was a timeline of photos at every age in school starting with kindergarten. In the first three his hand was visible and looked fine, but once I got to his second grade picture, it was obvious great effort had been made to conceal it. And there was something else. The boy no longer smiled as he had in the first couple of pictures. He looked solemn and detached. I turned a few more pages and immediately recognized the photo before me. I'd seen it at the art institute earlier that day. Thoughts flooded my mind, and I couldn't tear my eyes away from it. The girl in the painting hadn't been a girl at all—it was a boy.

"What are you really doing here?" a voice said from behind me.

The woman who first greeted me at the front door stood in the doorway. She'd been so quiet, I hadn't heard her approach.

"I'm sorry," I said. "I was just—"

She shook her head at me and entered the room.

"There's no need for excuses, dear. But I would like to know the real reason you're here."

"What's your relationship to Decklan?" I said. "I can

tell you're related in some way."

"I'm his mother. And," she said, pointing to the album I still clutched in my hand, "I'm that boy's grandmother."

CHAPTER 43

"He always hit every target he aimed at," the old woman said about the photo of the boy with the dead animal. "Won his first award when he was ten. I've never seen anyone who could hit a bull's eye the way he could."

"What's his name?" I said.

"What's yours?"

"Sloane."

"And you're a PI?"

I nodded.

She sat down on the bed and placed one hand behind her to brace herself.

"I'm sorry, but I can't stand for long periods of time anymore. My back isn't what it used to be. Let's sit a minute and have a little chat woman to woman while the men run around like boys."

I sat a couple feet away from her on the bed.

"Do you know why I question the real reason you're

here?" she said.

I shook my head.

"No one has ever come looking for Laurel. Not a single person. Since the day she walked out the door, she hasn't been missed by anyone in this town."

"What happened?" I said.

"She up and left with another man when the boy was only seven. Now you tell me, what kind of mother does that to her child? Leaves him without so much as a note, a phone call, a visit? I'll tell you—the trampy kind. That woman was only interested in one thing since the day she set eyes on my son—herself. And she only cared about one thing: money."

"Then why'd she leave all this?" I said.

"She found money somewhere else."

"What about her son?"

"She never wanted my grandson from the moment she found out she was pregnant with him. She told Decklan kids weren't part of their deal, like a child was some sort of business transaction two people make with each other. It sickens me to think about it, even now. I was surprised she lasted seven years."

I'd never had children, but to think there were women out there who could abandon a child was unthinkable to me. I wondered what kind of world we lived in where so many women were desperate to have babies but couldn't, while others who were undeserving pumped them out like balls in a paintball gun, one right after the other. It didn't seem fair.

"That must have been a difficult time for your grandson," I said.

"It was hard on them both. My son gave that woman everything her heart desired. He built her that art studio downtown and gave her whatever she asked for. But, it's like I told him. Women like that are never happy. They wrestle with themselves all of their lives, and in the end after all he'd done, I was right. She still walked out."

"How did he take it when she left?"

"He didn't want to talk about it. He just focused on his work."

"And your grandson?" I said.

"He was never the same after she left. Poor boy."

"What do you mean?"

"You need to understand, my grandson was a quiet boy to begin with. And when that poor example of a woman up and left, it got worse. He'd lock himself in his room for hours. Turned out, he was writing her letters. He'd write her every day and beg her to come back. Decklan told him we had no place to send them, but the boy wrote the letters anyway. He'd created this fantasy, maybe it was his way to cope so he didn't have to face reality. When I *could* get him out of his room, he planted himself on the front porch and waited for her to drive up. He'd convinced himself that she would come back, and no one could make him believe any different. It amazed me how much he loved her. He didn't seem to notice that she didn't give a damn about him."

I took out the note Sinnerman left for me in the park and folded it so she couldn't see the words.

"By any chance did the paper he wrote on look like this?"

Her eyes scanned it and then widened such that I did not need a verbal answer.

"Where did you get that? Do you know my grandson—do you know where he is?"

I pressed harder.

"Is this the paper?" I said.

"Yes."

"How long has it been since you've seen your grandson?"

She tapped one of her fingers over her lips and then said, "I don't know. He left."

"How long ago?" I said.

"It's been years now, about two decades."

"Do you have any idea where he went?"

A tear oozed from her eye and splashed down on her wrist. She took her index finger and cocked her head to the side and dabbed the wet spot with it.

"Decklan set aside a big chunk of money for my grandson, which he was entitled to at the age of eighteen. The day after he turned eighteen, he took out his inheritance and left town. I've never seen him since."

"Have you tried to get in touch with him—to find him?"

She nodded.

"And?" I said.

"I have no idea where he is. Have you ever tried to find someone who doesn't want to be found?"

I had, and I'd learned no matter how hard someone tried to hide, there was always a trail.

"Couldn't you track him through his bank account, credit cards, that type of thing?" I said.

"He cashed it out."

"All of it?" I said.

"Every penny."

I had the feeling there was a lot more to the story, and I wasn't about to leave before I found out what it was.

"Why did your grandson want to leave so bad?" I said.

She shook her head.

"I'm sorry, I can't. Even after all this time, it's just too hard."

It was time for the sympathy vote, but I didn't have the heart to tell her about my suspicions.

"You asked me before why I was here," I said.

She nodded.

"I'm looking for your grandson."

"Why?"

"I think he knew my sister," I said. "In fact, I believe he might have been the last one to see her alive."

Giovanni and Decklan appeared at the door.

"What are you two talking about?" Decklan said.

I gave Giovanni the I-*need-more-time* look, hoping he would grasp my meaning. He did.

"I'd love to see the rest of this magnificent house," he said to Decklan.

Decklan's house paled in comparison to Giovanni's, but Decklan took the bait, which was all that mattered. When they were safely out of sight, Decklan's mother grabbed my arm.

"Is your sister—"

"Yes," I said.

"How long ago did she pass away?"

"A few years."

"I'm sorry."

"Me too." I said. "I hope you can see now why I need to find him."

"How are you so sure the man you're looking for is my grandson?"

"Because he wrote me a note on the same type of paper I showed you, and I believe his mother's art studio was the only place around that used it."

"I see."

"What made him leave?" I said.

She sighed and then breathed in and exhaled with

force, like she was prepared to give a long speech.

"Decklan had a hard time after Laurel left. He didn't sleep, he didn't eat. All he thought about was her. And you need to understand that every time he looked at my grandson, he saw Laurel staring back at him. It pained him to even talk to the child. At first, he just distanced himself from him, but after a while, just to have him around was more than he could bear."

"So he ignored him—his own son?"

She hung her head, as if disgraced.

"Decklan sent him away."

"Where, at what age?"

"To an all-boy school about three months after his mother left, and when he came back, he was like a different person."

"In what way?" I said.

"He had fits of rage and night terrors. He'd wake up at all hours and scream for his mother. This went on for years. He was so angry."

"How did Decklan react?"

"He didn't know what to do. I'm sure he loved the boy, but you have to understand, he's never had a high tolerance for that type of behavior."

That type of behavior? I couldn't believe she'd uttered those words. The child lost his mother. How could his father expect anything less?

"And he was violent," she said. "The older he got, the

worse it was, and it escalated until he went after Decklan one night with a knife."

"Was he hurt?" I said.

She shook her head.

"It was more rage than anything. He thought his father hated him, and by then—well, he pretty much assumed his mother felt the same way too. All those years, and he never heard a word from her. But the night he got physical with the knife—well, that was the last straw for Decklan."

"How old was your grandson when this all happened?" I said.

"Sixteen. Decklan gave him some money and said he'd pay for him to have a place of his own and all of his expenses, on one condition."

"Which was?"

"He left and never came back."

The entire story was unreal, and I felt like I was in an episode of *The Twilight Zone*. I couldn't believe a father could do that to his own son.

"And did he—leave I mean?"

She nodded.

"I kept in touch with him and visited him at the place his father set up for him, and I begged Decklan to take him back. He needed his father. But both of them were too proud to even speak to the other. And that's how I lost him."

"What happened to his hand?" I said.

"Burned himself on the stove when he was a little boy. He used to light things on fire over the burner. When I asked him about it he said he liked to watch things melt down into ash. It drove his father crazy, but he still did it whenever he wasn't around. And then one day it got out of control, and when he tried to put it out, he lit his own hand on fire."

"Where was Decklan during all this?"

"I'm embarrassed to say the boy was home alone, but I didn't live here then. He called 9-1-1 himself and was taken to the hospital. By the time Decklan arrived, child services had arrived. I thought they would take him, and I was relieved when they didn't. Sometimes I wonder if he might have been better off if they had."

I went to close the photo album and return it to its rightful place when I noticed a pocket attached to the back cover. A picture protruded from it. I pulled it out and stared into the face of a young, brunette woman.

"That's her," the woman said.

"Laurel?" I said.

She nodded.

Laurel looked a lot like Sinnerman's victims. Dark hair, dark eyes, slender, same age group—I was astonished.

"I appreciate you taking the time to talk to me," I said.

"I don't know how any of this helps you, but if you

do find my Samuel, will you tell him how much I've missed him all these years? It would mean everything to me if I could see him again."

A couple things stood out most in our conversation. Sinnerman strangled his victims with most of his force applied with his right hand. The left was weak and made strange looking imprints on the bodies. The burns from the stove made sense. And then there was the comment about him being able to shoot at a target with impeccable accuracy.

I thanked her again and then asked if I could use the restroom before I left. I'd seen what appeared to be the corner of a notebook stowed away under the dust ruffle of the bed. Once she exited the bedroom I went back in, snatched it and plunged it into my bag. As I left the room, I looked back at the picture of the child with the fish on the dresser, but I no longer saw an innocent little boy—I saw the face of a killer.

CHAPTER 44

We reached the car and Decklan waved farewell to Giovanni, his newfound friend, and then went around to the side of the house and gazed at the monstrosity of daisies in his flower bed.

I turned to Giovanni and said, "I'll be right back, okay?"

"Do you want me to accompany you?"

I shook my head.

"I need a moment alone with Decklan."

I tossed my handbag in the car and shut the door and made my way over to him.

"I just want you to know that you disgust me," I said.

Decklan turned around with a dumfounded look on his face. He turned to the left and then the right, like he thought my words were meant for someone else.

"Excuse me?"

"Why did you turn your back on your son?" I said.

"After all he'd been through with the loss of his mother, I'd love for you to explain to me how a person justifies doing what you did."

"You're out of line."

"Of the two of us, Mr. Reids, I assure you, the only person out of line here is you."

The   out-of-the-ballpark-and-never-going-to-return kind of out.

"You don't understand, my son was—"

"Tore up when his mother left, I know," I said. "So were you. That doesn't give you the right to shun him."

"You could never understand."

"He was angry, hurt, frustrated, and he needed help. What's not to get? And you could have gotten him the help he needed, but instead you chose to abandon him, which makes *you* responsible."

"For what? I don't know what kind of stories my mother filled your head with, but Samuel made his own choice to disassociate from this family. He was more than happy to do so. It was what he wanted."

"And what about you?" I said. "It's easy to shift the blame to your son, but you're the one who asked him to leave and never to come back."

"It was his decision, and he made it."

"You talk about it like you gave him a choice. Cut the crap, Mr. Reids. We both know you didn't."

Decklan plunged the hoe he held in his hand deep

into the terra firma with great force. "Enough! How dare you come to my home and assume to know anything."

"You have no idea," I said. "Not the first clue about the man your son is today."

Decklan took three steps toward me. He was too close. It made me uncomfortable. It violated my inner circle of trust. A circle he wasn't in, not by a long shot, and before I knew it he'd lifted his hand in the air. Giovanni was out of the car and by my side in a flash.

"Back up out of my face," I said.

"Or what?" Decklan said to Giovanni. "You need to get a handle on your woman."

I still had a lot to learn about Giovanni, but one thing I knew without a doubt was that no one spoke to him that way and got away with it. I held my hand out to Giovanni to indicate I still had more welled up inside me. He grimaced but remained by my side in silence.

I turned to Decklan. "You won't understand this right now, but one day you will—I blame your son for his actions—there's no excuse for the person he's allowed himself to become. But you, Mr. Reids, will someday have to own your part in all of it. You weren't there when he needed you most, and whether you realize it now or later, at some point you'll never be able to forgive yourself."

Decklan stood still with his jaw propped open wide enough for a little bird to fly in and forge a nest. He wanted to say something, but there were no words. All he managed was a pathetic, "Get off my lawn."

Weak.

"And now I need a moment," Giovanni said.

"Let's just go," I said.

Giovanni put his hand on my shoulder. "Sloane, I'll meet you at the car."

I thought about fighting it, but I knew he'd given me my moment to shine and he deserved to have his if he wanted it, though I couldn't imagine what more needed to be said.

On my way back to the car, Giovanni sounded off in the distance. I didn't hear all of what he said, but it started something like: "If you ever come at her like that again, I'll—" It got me wondering what I missed after that. I'll break your fingers? I'll string you up and dangle you from the edge of the top of a hotel? Or maybe it was something more gangster like: I'll bust a cap in your ass. All I knew was I had a protective guard dog that allowed me to do pretty much whatever I wanted, and since we'd met, he'd always been there to back me up. I liked my independence, but I couldn't deny the fact that it was nice to feel protected at the same time. Woof.

CHAPTER 45

Sam Reids sat on a somewhat gnarled but thick wooden branch of a tree in his yard; a yard located one street over from Decklan Reid's house. Through his binoculars he watched Sloane scold his father and then some strange man he'd never seen before follow suit. The strange man angered him. He stood close to Sloane. Too close.

Sam's attempt to control his emotions had subsided about an hour earlier when Sloane entered his childhood home and then his room. Her lack of respect filled him with rage. He hadn't foreseen her level of commitment or what Decklan and his grandmother would tell her about who he was and what had become of him. It didn't matter. What could they possibly know?

Sam felt like he should care, but he didn't. Only one thing mattered to him now: Sloane. They could say whatever they wanted. If his own father was too stupid to recognize him when he drove by in his car day after day,

Sam was sure any information his father offered the authorities wouldn't make the least bit of difference. They wouldn't be able to track down his whereabouts. It wasn't like they'd ever tried anyway. Sam recalled the time he rolled by Decklan on a side street, and Decklan actually waved a friendly hello, all the while being too stupid to recognize it was his own son. It had been over two decades, of course, but just for a split second Sam thought Decklan would be able to identify him for who he was—his son. Except now Sam didn't see himself like that at all anymore. He wasn't Decklan's son; he was Sam. And his father wasn't his father—not anymore.

Sam had purchased the home on the next street when he learned his grandmother moved in with Decklan. She was frail, and there wasn't much life left in her now, and she needed someone to help look after her. Not that Decklan was the one for the job. Sam was sure it was the other way around and that her moving in would take years from her life instead of adding to them. Sam watched her sit on his old bed for hours, poring over the old photo album. Sometimes she would cry and clutch the album tight to her heart. He liked to see her distraught and unhappy. At least someone missed him.

Today was the first time Sam felt different about his grandmother. He watched her talking to Sloane and was desperate to know what she'd said. He didn't like the way it made him feel—like he'd cut himself at a crime scene and left splotches of blood behind. He tried not to panic when Sloane had snuck back into his room and stole his old notebook—the one he wished he hadn't left behind. It hadn't mattered until now. No one had ever seemed to notice it was even there. And now Sloane had come along and abducted it from its place of eternal rest. It was unforgivable. How could she defile him that way? Those were his private thoughts, the ones no one else should ever see. She needed to be punished.

CHAPTER 46

"Did you get any information from the old woman?" Giovanni said.

I spent the next several minutes going over what Sinnerman's grandmother told me and my theory about who he was.

When I finished he said, "Are you certain about this?"

I nodded.

"That boy's our killer," I said. "Only he isn't a little boy anymore. I don't envy his poor upbringing or what he must have suffered as a child, but it doesn't excuse him from his actions. You can't just go around killing people because you hate your mother and the rest of the world."

"So where to now?" Giovanni said.

"I'm sure I won't score any points with your brother for what I've done, but he needs to know what we found out."

*****

We parked in front of the last place I wanted to be, and I hoped the backlash of not letting them in on what we'd been doing wouldn't bite me too hard in the ass. If it did, I didn't care. It was worth it.

I pulled the notebook from my bag.

"What have you got there?" Giovanni said.

"I found this in the boy's room. I didn't want to hand it over until I'd had a chance to look through it."

"They'll want it."

"I know," I said. "I've only had the chance to flip through the pages, but it looks like a bunch of scribbled words."

"Shove it under the seat," Giovanni said.

"What?"

"Do it—now."

I did what he said, and five seconds later, Giovanni's brother tapped on the driver-side window.

"What are you two doing here?" Agent Luciana said.

"Came to see if you had dinner yet."

"I haven't."

"Care to join us?" Giovanni said.

"Sure. Let me grab something from my car, and we'll go."

"I need to run Sloane somewhere," Giovanni said. "Can you meet us in thirty minutes?"

We set up a place for dinner and then said goodbye.

"Thanks for the quick save," I said when we were

alone again.

"I didn't mean to be so firm with you, but there wasn't time to mince words."

"I would have done the same thing," I said and winked at him. "Let's run this errand."

Giovanni took me to the local office supply store, and I photocopied all the pages in the notebook. Ten minutes later, we took our places next to Agent Luciana on the patio of my favorite restaurant in Kimball Junction.

"What have you two been up to?" he said.

Giovanni crossed one leg over the other and behaved like we were a few old friends just passing the time with a casual dinner. I wondered how he stayed so calm all the time. I felt like a freight train was trying to pass through me, and I just wanted to pull on the horn and blurt it all out, consequences or no.

"I know who Sinnerman is," I said.

I hadn't meant to put myself on blast, but now I'd released it, and there was nothing left to do but press on. Giovanni glanced over to the side at nothing, but I could see the smirk on his face.

"You're not serious?" Agent Luciana said.

"I assure you, she is," Giovanni said.

"Are you going to tell me what the two of you have been up to, or do you expect me to guess?"

I explained the series of events which started with the discovery of the pink paper at the art school and ended with our trip to Decklan Reids' house.

"I can't believe you, either of you."

"I failed to see the value in dispersing the details until we had something solid to give you," Giovanni said.

"This is my investigation, Gio. I mean, it's great you like this girl, but you don't need to lose your head over her."

Giovanni slammed his hand down on the table. Fragments of bread crumbs shot through the air, landing on the pavement below.

"Watch yourself, brother," Giovanni said.

The two stared each other down for what seemed like a full five minutes even though it couldn't have been more than one. I'd watched a dog training show once on TV where I learned that in order to establish dominance when engaged in a stare-off, as these two were doing now, never to be the first one to look away; it signaled weakness. The one who held the stare without breaking first became the dominant, the leader. And Agent Luciana might have been angry, but he and I both knew who would be the first one to look away.

Several seconds later, Agent Luciana turned toward me.

"Can you understand why I'm frustrated?"

I nodded.

"I expected it. I never meant to disregard you or your position; I just—"

"Can't help yourself?" Agent Luciana said.

"I know I jump the gun sometimes, but in the past I've always felt like everyone wanted to know what information I had, but once I gave it, I was rewarded by being ushered to the sidelines. All that sitting has made my butt sore, and I can't sit back—not on this one."

"I'm not like every detective you've worked with," Agent Luciana said. "Maybe if you gave me a chance, you'd know you could trust me."

"That's just it," I said. "I don't trust anyone."

"What you've told me gives me a lot to look into, but we're still talking about a simple piece of paper here. There's no other evidence the Reids's boy is our killer."

I reached down and picked up the notebook and plopped it down on the tablecloth in front of him.

"There's this," I said.

I waited for the backlash I was sure would ensue, but it didn't.

"Where'd you find it?" Agent Luciana said.

"In the boy's room. No one else knew it was there. It was so dusty when I picked it up, I couldn't even tell what color it was at first. I hope you can use it."

CHAPTER 47

After dinner was over, Agent Luciana got a warrant to search Decklan Reids's house which I'm sure came as a shock to both Decklan and his mother.

Surprise—your son grew up to be a fine serial killer, well done, nice job. You don't just deserve a pat on the back for your achievements in the non-parenting category, you deserve two. Wait a minute while I find my bat and then we'll toast to Decklan and Laurel, parents of the year—thirty-plus years running.

There was this itch I'd tried not to scratch since I left Decklan's house, an urge to find Samuel's mother and tell her what her son had become. It passed. I knew my focus was on Sinnerman, and if I still felt the need once I'd found him, I'd make my decision then.

I sat back on the bed and bent open the copies I'd printed from the notebook. Its passages alarmed me.

My birth was undesirable to her. I wasn't meant to

come into this world.

She's dead to me like I am dead to her. Rest in peace Laurel, rest in peacc.

I know why you didn't want to have me. I don't belong here. I think of things I am going to do in my mind. Not to you Laurel, but because of you. You drove me to it. You made me, and one day I will show you and the rest of the world what I can do.

When I look at a woman, I only see her hair. Your hair. You sat in front of your mirror and brushed it for hours. Time you could have spent with me.

It's what I have to do, and what it's telling me to do inside me, inside my mind. It's saying 'you deserve this.' I want it to go out of my mind, but it can't.

I broke the windows in Laurel's art studio today. I threw rocks and then I watched them shatter. Dad is mad, but he doesn't know I did it, and he'll never know because he's too stupid to think it was me. And then I went to the store and stole some stuff. I just picked out what I wanted and put it in my pocket. It was so easy. I didn't even need it, I just wanted to do it because no one was watching and I could. I am starting to think I can do anything.

People will believe anything, especially girls. They're so easy to manipulate. They seem so innocent, but they aren't. They act like they're nice, but just wait until they grow up and have babies. Babies they'll give away because they can, or maybe they'll keep them for a while and then leave, just like Laurel did.

Everyone in my school wants to be me because I get into the most trouble and I show them all how to do it, how to prank, steal and get away with anything. I'm their king, the person they all look to. They're my minions and I'm their leader. I'll lead and you follow, I say. And it works every time.

My head hurts all the time and I can't ever sleep. I lie awake in my room at night and think about things I shouldn't be thinking about and sometimes I wonder if I'm no longer in control of my mind. I'm going to take a tire iron to my dad's car tomorrow and tell him I saw the kid down the street do it. He doesn't care about me; he only cares about his money.

I hid around a corner today while my dad was talking to my gran about me. He said I had to go, and she said I could come and live at her house. He said no. He would give me money like he always had and be done with me. He was never a father to me anyway so I'll take it and I'll never come back. Neither one of them will ever see me again.

Yea, the light of the wicked shall be put out and the spark of his fire shall not shine. Job 18 and 5.

When I read the last passage, all I could think about was how the light of the wicked would be put out. The difference was, that light would be his, and I planned to be the one to put it out—forever.

I folded the pages and stuck them in the side-table drawer and then wandered through the house. I found Giovanni outside on his back deck with a Robert B. Parker novel in his hand and Lord Berkeley at rest by his side. There was something different about Lord Berkeley though. Someone had dressed him up in a double-breasted suit with a velvet jacket over the top. He looked ridiculous and hot, and I imagined any minute he would turn around and say that Holmes was his new name and ask me to call him Sherlock.

I tried not to show my disapproval and faced Giovanni and said, "I didn't know you liked to read."

He folded the cover flap over a page and looked up at me.

"There's a lot you don't know about me."

That was an understatement.

He assessed Lord Berkeley and said, "Not my idea. It was my sister. She couldn't help herself. I can pull it off if you like; I can tell you're not a fan."

"I'm sure it cost her a fortune, so I expect it will be fine to leave it on him a little longer. What are you reading?"

"*Looking for Rachel Wallace*. I've found myself

rereading some of his old works since he passed last year."

"I like period novels—Austen, Bronte, Dickens, that type of thing," I said. "I've collected books for years."

"A fellow reader. We have more in common all the time."

I sat down beside him.

"I feel like there's still so much I don't know about you. It's strange just being here. I mean, we've only really known each other for a couple weeks."

He leaned forward and said, "What is it you'd like to know—you can ask me anything."

I couldn't refuse.

"I've watched you around your brother, with the men lurking around here, and you have this massive house with all kinds of security. It seems everyone looks to you for answers, and then there's your car and all this other stuff you own, and every room in this house is decorated with expensive things, and you—"

He reached for my hand and folded it inside both of his.

"What do you want to ask me?"

I wanted to take five and prolong the moment, but I knew it was time.

"Are you the head person, like a boss guy—some kind of don or something? I've seen stuff on TV, but you don't wear a ring, and in the movies the people kiss the ring, and since you don't have one, I don't know if I'm crazy, or…"

I felt so stupid when the words poured out of my mouth, and the constant twitch in my leg wasn't helping things either.

He released my hand and leaned back and acted like I'd just asked him how he took his coffee.

"I have many people I look after, including my own family—but no ring."

I guessed it was his way of saying: *Yes, Sloane, I'm a mafia boss. I dabble in mafia affairs. Can I bump off someone for you?*

He continued.

"I'm involved in a handful of businesses, and I use the money I've earned over the years for many things." He stretched his arm out all the way and said, "Come with me. I'd like to show you something.

*****

An hour later we were parked outside a building in downtown Salt Lake City.

"What is this place?" I said.

"A shelter for women and children."

I looked around. It didn't look like any shelter I'd ever seen. The building itself was a work of art. The outside was so luminescent, it glowed. The building towered above the others in the area. The flower beds that surrounded all four sides of the building were immaculate and filled with rich shades of purple, pink, blue, and white. They reminded me of the atrium at Bellagio in Las Vegas. The smell of honeysuckle penetrated the air. I stood a moment and appreciated the beauty that radiated from all sides before I walked by two Italians dressed up as security guards and followed Giovanni inside.

When I walked through the door I heard, "Mr. Luciana. Good to see you again."

"And you, Rochelle." He faced me. "This is Sloane. I'll be showing her around."

She nodded and then retreated behind a desk in the center of the room.

"Do people always let you do whatever you want?" I said.

He smiled and said, "Most of the time, yes. But it helps when you own the place."

We walked into the different areas of the facility, and in fifteen minutes, I'd seen enough to last a lifetime: women with blackened eyes, children on crutches, some with broken arms or legs. Some walked around freely while others were downtrodden and stuck to their beds.

"What happens to them here?"

"They are treated, and they are safe. It's a refuge. A place where they can't be harmed."

"How long do they stay?"

"Depends on their needs, and those of their children. My goal in building this place was to get them back on their feet and then to offer counseling. I offer the chance of a better life. All they need to do is embrace it. In here they are taught essential skills like self-defense, and they are given the tools they need so that when they are ready to leave, they can survive anything."

"This place and what you are doing—it's amazing," I said. "These women owe you their lives."

"I know what it feels like to be the one someone puts the screws to. I've witnessed and suffered through many things in my life, even as a child, and this is my opportunity to make it better. Even if it makes only the smallest impact on humankind. It will spread to future generations that come along after I'm long gone. A single piece of grain can make all the difference in the world if you nurture it."

I stood there in that moment with a full heart and in complete awe of him.

In the corner of the room, a young boy looked our direction and then darted into the next room and returned seconds later with a group of children. They ran to Giovanni, and he bent down to greet them.

"Gio, Gio," they said. "Will you read us a story?"

"Please," one girl said.

"Double please," said another.

Giovanni laughed and said, "All right then, one story

and then it's bedtime. Go and choose a book for me to read."

A minute later we were in a room full of beanbags with an assortment of children who latched on to every word Giovanni read like a room full of parishioners listening to a sermon.

There were times in my life when I felt like I was a magnet to all things complicated. Giovanni seemed stable and secure and more magnificent than I expected him to be. Here he was in a safe house with a book in his hand reading to a handful of children. There was just one caveat that played like a skipped record in the back of my mind, and there was no getting around it. I was dating a modern version of Don Corleone, and as impressive as the safe house was, there were two sides to a man like this. There had to be.

CHAPTER 48

In the morning I found a note next to my bed suggesting I go upstairs, walk to the second door on the right, and go in. I'd never been one to back down from a good old fashioned surprise, and I wasn't about to now either.

Lord Berkeley was still asleep on the bed next to me sans his detective costume, so I slipped out the side of the bed, wrapped a robe around me, and tiptoed out to the hall. When I arrived at the door in question, I imagined what I might possibly find on the other side. I almost didn't want to open the oversized double doors, in fear I would spoil what I'd built up in my mind.

I grabbed both knobs in my hands and pushed them open at the same time and then gasped. Along the walls on all four sides of the room were bookshelves lined with books—old, new, collectible—they were all there, and there were thousands of them. A desk in the middle of the room contained a note with my name written on the front. I opened it.

Sloane, read whatever you wish. I hope this helps take your mind off things.

I folded it and slipped it inside the pocket of my robe.

"Amazing, isn't it?"

I spun around to see Giovanni's sister at the door.

"Morning," I said.

"He's been collecting for over twenty years now. It's a big deal he let you in this room, you know."

"What do you mean?"

"This is where he comes for refuge, and usually when he's in here, everyone knows he's not to be disturbed."

"I see. He showed me the shelter last night. What he's doing, it's wonderful."

Daniela laughed.

"He's, ah, built ten of them. He puts others before himself all the time."

"I agree," I said.

"Listen, I have to head out."

"So soon?" I said.

"It's time for me to get back to my real life. I just came up here to say goodbye."

She had a look on her face that said something more.

"And?"

"Don't hurt my brother."

"What makes you think I would?" I said.

"I can't remember the last time he had a girlfriend. He's cautious with women; most don't appeal to him."

"Why?"

"They can't think for themselves, are interested in his money. So it's rare for him to attach himself to anyone. As his girlfriend, I thought you should know."

"But I'm not his—"

"Of course you are. Just don't hurt him. He acts all tough, and believe me, he is, but he's let you see the other side of him, and not many do, so consider yourself lucky."

She walked over and squeezed me tight. "See you soon."

I selected an old copy of *Jane Eyre*. I walked down the stairs and was met by Giovanni.

"I was just coming to find you," he said.

"You have quite the book collection. I could have spent hours in there. I've never seen anything like it, thank you for—"

He grabbed my arms and shook me, not hard—but enough to get my attention.

"Sloane."

I looked into his eyes. Something wasn't right.

"What's happened?" I said.

"How fast can you get ready?"

CHAPTER 49

It wasn't time for the first matinee of the day at the local movie theater, and already there were two patrons. The only thing was—they were both dead. The garbage collector noticed them when he made his early morning rounds and called it in. Two women, fully clothed, were spread out on the ground in front of the theater for all to see. They were side by side with one arm across their chest and the other spread out, just like the other victims had been. Their right hands had been hacked off, and one had Sinnerman's signature S carved in her wrist, but the other girl had something different carved in her wrist, an M.

Maddie had called Sloane at the first opportunity.

"Maybe he's breaking up his name into two words now," Maddie said on the phone, "since there's two women. One for Sinner and the other for Man. This is the first time he's killed more than one at the same time."

"Or it could stand for something else."

"Oh please, you're being ridiculous."

"Am I? Those initials could be mine too."

"How close are you?" Maddie said.

"ETA is five minutes."

"The place is already swarming with fed's and everyone else on the planet, so I'm not sure how close you'll be able to get to the victims."

"If Coop's there, I'm sure I won't get anywhere near them."

"Here's hoping he's down with some kind of tragic illness where he needs bed rest," Maddie said.

I pressed the end button on my phone and looked at Giovanni.

"Every time someone is killed, I can't help but feel it's my fault," I said.

He took his right hand off the wheel, replacing it with his left, and then reached over and set his hand on top of mine.

"You can't think like that."

"It's hard not to. And I feel like I've let my sister down because I still haven't found this guy. All I do is keep sending others to join her."

"We will catch him, and he'll pay for what he's done, and you will be the one to be congratulated for it. If not for you, the feds wouldn't have the information they have now."

We parked across the theater and exited the car, but Coop was ready and waiting.

"You shouldn't be here," Coop said.

"I have every right. What have you done recently? Not a damn thing from what I can see, so don't try and tell me about what I'm entitled to and what I'm not."

Once I'd said it, I actually felt bad. Coop was silent for a moment, which was rare for him. He'd worked just as hard on the case as I had the first time around and never even turned over one rock that gave him a solid lead on the killer.

Coop made a motion with his hand like he was trying to swat a fly in my direction and walked off. It wasn't like him to back down from me, and a minute later I realized he hadn't. The chief headed straight for me and said, "You know you shouldn't be here, Sloane."

"After everything? You're still going to keep me behind some ridiculous line like I'm a spectator?"

The chief gave a courtesy nod to Giovanni and said, "Mind if I borrow her a minute?" like I was some car at a rental agency. He pulled me by the arm over to the side.

"Listen, we've been down this road many times before, and you know I need you to keep your distance so we can do our job. Now I know Giovanni has some kind of magical muscle he seems to flex over his brother, and I've no doubt that he could get you in here, so I'm asking you to respect me here and not to push it."

I opened my mouth to speak, and he leaned in even closer and said, "Besides, I know Madison will get you down to her office the first chance she gets, and you can examine the bodies there."

"It's not the same as searching the scene."

"We're doing that," the chief said.

"I meant, myself."

"I'm asking you to trust me on this."

I was stunned. In all our years together the chief had never *asked* me to do anything. He *told* me and expected me to comply with any and all requests. I really did have more power with Giovanni by my side.

Maddie and her platinum pigtails approached us from the side. "What's up?"

Neither of us spoke.

"I can see I've barged in on you two, so—"

She turned to go and I said, "Maddie, wait."

I caught up to her. "The chief doesn't want me close to the bodies."

"Shocker."

"Yeah, but there's something else," I said.

"What do you mean?"

"He took the time to drag me aside and talk to me about it, and I detected something in his voice—it was like he was nervous."

"Hmmm, I don't know."

"See what you can find out for me, okay?" I said.

"You got it."

She leaned in close and whispered, "Meet me at my office in three and you can examine the bodies there."

I watched Maddie cross over to the dark side, slip plastic gloves on her hands, and hunch over the bodies. Ten seconds later, she was writing in a furious motion in her notebook, and I was removing myself from the scene.

*****

The look on Maddie's face when I walked into her lab was that of a doctor preparing to give news to a family about the death of their loved one.

"What is it?" I said.

"What?"

"Maddie, come on."

"I don't know what you're talking about."

"Really? You haven't looked this sad since you found out *All My Children* was going off the air."

I could count on one hand the amount of times I'd seen Maddie forlorn over the years. Most of her life had been spent living in some blissful bubble no matter what happened around her.

"What have you found?" I said.

She shook her head.

"You'll tell me sooner or later, so how about you just get whatever it is off your chest."

"There was a note."

"The same kind Sinnerman always leaves?" I said.

She nodded.

"What did it say?"

"Wade doesn't want me to talk to you about it."

"Since when have we allowed a man to come between us?"

She backed up against the counter and sighed.

"It's just that the note was for you."

I sighed. "I appreciate the two of you being considerate of my feelings, but I don't need protection right now—I need answers."

She shrugged and said, "Fine. It said: Hello, Sloane Monroe. See what you made me do?"

CHAPTER 50

"That's it?" I said. "The whole thing?"

Maddie nodded.

"All right."

"Are you okay?"

"Why wouldn't I be?" I said.

"Turn around and look in that mirror behind you."

I revolved around and looked at myself in the mirror behind me.

"What?" I said.

"You're gnawing away at the inside of your cheek like you always do when your anxiety gets the best of you."

I stopped.

"I'm fine."

I wanted to be fine and shake off the sense of responsibility I felt for every murder Sinnerman committed since he'd started again. I'd failed all of them.

I had three years to produce the killer while everyone else sat idly by and did nothing, and I might as well have sat right along with them.

"This is why I didn't want to tell you," Maddie said.

"He can say whatever he likes. It just incites me to find him all the more. I'm ready to take a look at the bodies."

We walked into the next room, and my eyes focused in on one thing, and that was all it took—I was distracted. I picked up one of the silver tools from Maddie's mess of a tray and suddenly had the urge to rearrange everything. I took the three shortest ones and placed them on the left and continued to sort by size, until a hand reached in and slapped me on the wrist.

"Check your OCD at the door," Maddie said. "You're in my lab now, and I don't need you making a mess of my tools."

"Do you see how you have them arranged on here? I don't know how you find anything."

Maddie grabbed a random tool and angled it at me.

"Everything's just the way I like it, so back off, sister."

I stepped back. "What have you found out so far?"

Maddie walked over to both women and stood between them.

"This one here with the S carved into her wrist went first and fast. He choked her out and then strangled her. I didn't find any signs of a struggle, and she had no lacerations anywhere else on her body. It was like he picked her up, sedated and killed her in a hurry, and then moved on to the next one."

She turned to the second victim and said, "This one wasn't so lucky."

"I'm afraid to ask."

"He took more time with her, and she was killed in a style similar to the other women. She had three lacerations on her left leg, and see this impression right under her upper arm?"

I nodded.

"It's the shape and size of a thumb print, and it looks like he pressed it into her for some reason—hard."

Maddie looked at both girls.

"There is one difference between these women and the others. Their hair is lighter than all the other vics."

"I noticed," I said. "Maybe it was quantity and not quality he was after this time."

"Both girls have been identified, and it turns out they knew each other. They were best friends."

CHAPTER 51

Sam Reids hovered over his shelves and admired the recent additions to his trophies on the second row. There was something about the hands that mesmerized him more than the fingers he'd collected. Every now and then he swore they swayed in their liquid coffins and waved at him.

He wondered what Sloane thought of the note he left at the crime scene and if she cringed when she saw it. By now the anger and denial he had over the five-finger discount she'd done on his notebook had subsided and was replaced with a sense of relief and acceptance—something he never thought possible. He arched his back, folded his arms, and imagined Sloane in a quiet room with nothing but his words to keep her company. Now she would understand him like no one ever had, and their relationship would be forever changed.

Sam's favorite song blared through the speakers of

his Bose iPod dock. He hummed the soft melody and leaned back and allowed himself to return to a previous time in his life, where he found himself alone in a stark-white room with Laurel. He was five and she was—well, significantly older. How much so Sam didn't know at the time. He just knew she looked like a mom, even though she didn't act like one. Laurel knelt down next to him, and her soft hair fell in his face. It smelled like he'd dipped his hand in a jar of honey.

"What's this song called, Mommy?" Sam said.

"Sinnerman."

Sam didn't know what that meant.

"Who's the singer?"

"Nina Simone."

He liked the name Nina but didn't care much for Simone.

"Why does he have two first names?"

"Not he silly, she."

Sam thought Nina didn't sound like a woman at all. Her voice was low and rough, like a man's.

"What's it about?" he said.

Laurel knelt down and extended her right hand and pulled her fingers back toward herself. "Come here," she said to Sam. "You want to hear a story?"

Sam nodded. Laurel never told him stories. It made him feel special. He walked over and knelt by her side.

"When Nina Simone was little, she used to go to church with her mama, who was a Methodist," Laurel said.

"What's a Messosist?"

Laurel placed a finger in the middle of Sam's lips. "Shhh," she said. "Do you want to hear the story or not?"

He nodded.

"Well then, shush now."

Laurel continued.

"Nina's mama was a minister at that church, and they used to sing this song to help sway people into confessing their sins."

Sam was confused. He didn't know what "sway" or "confess" meant, but he knew if he asked, he might never hear the rest of the story.

"When Nina grew up, she became a famous singer, and she remembered this song and decided to sing it for the whole world to hear. Do you want to know what I think the song means?"

Sam nodded and clung to her every word.

"There was a man and his name was Sinnerman, and he spent his life running around doing bad things until one day he woke up and realized what he'd done, and he was ashamed. He didn't like who he was anymore, and all he wanted to do was to run and hide. So he went out and tried to find a place where he could shield himself from the rest of the world, and he looked for someone to

*take him in. Only, no one wanted him. They'd all heard
about this man called Sinnerman, and they thought he
was no good. So they shut him out, and with no place to
go, he sought out the Lord. But the Lord had seen all the
things Sinnerman had done, and He told him he couldn't
stay. He said there was only one place for him, and He
pointed Sinnerman in the direction that he must go."*

"Where?"

"He was sent to live with the devil."

The song ended, and Sam snapped back to reality. He
didn't like to think about Laurel or the life he used to
have. His past had wasted away, and any emotions he'd
ever possessed corroded along with it. Whether he lived
or died mattered little to him now. He knew it would all
come to an end regardless.

A female voice from the other room cried out in
terror, and Sam rose from his chair and looked at the
clock on the wall. The drugs had worn off. He didn't like
it when they talked. It made them seem so real, so human.
He preferred them quiet. He grabbed a knife from the
counter, walked to the room she was in, and closed the
door behind him.

CHAPTER 52

Agent Luciana and the chief sat on the corner of Kearns and Main.

"Where's Giovanni?" Agent Luciana said when I drove up.

"Busy," I said. "What have you found out?"

"The handwriting in the notebook is a match to the Sinnerman letters," the chief said. "Almost exact even though I assume he wrote those journal entries years ago, but his style hasn't changed much over the years."

"You're sure?"

Agent Luciana nodded. "Without a doubt."

"And the prints?"

The chief shook his head.

"We only found yours."

"How's that possible?"

He shrugged his shoulders and said, "Don't know, but it had been wiped down."

"Now what?" I said. "Am I the only one who feels like we take two steps forward and three steps back?"

"We've come a long way since I arrived," Agent Luciana said. "We're close, I can feel it. Pops and grandma are on their way in for questioning, and I've got my team on standby. Once they're out of the house, we'll sweep the whole thing."

I thought about his grandmother and how it would affect her when she found out.

"I have a request."

The chief rolled his eyes.

"Why am I not surprised?" he said.

"I'd like to talk with the grandmother for a moment before you guys get started."

"Not a good idea," Agent Luciana said.

"Look, I've already spoken to her once, and believe me when I say the news of her grandson being a killer isn't going to be easy for her to take. It would be better coming from me, and then you can take over and ask her all the questions you want. It won't get you anywhere, but if that's the way you want to go—it's not like I can stop you."

"We'll go easy on her. It's not necessary for you to be there," Agent Luciana said.

The inside of my body felt like it was in a tepid room and someone had just cranked up the heat as high as it would go.

"Neither of you would be where you are on this case if it wasn't for me; maybe you both should take that into consideration. If anyone can get through to her it's me. So let's not sit here and waste more time going round and round with this."

Breathe, Sloane, breathe, I told myself. *Count to fifty if you have to, but don't lose it!*

Agent Luciana turned to the chief who threw his hands up. I'd won.

*****

"Sloane, I don't understand what this is all about—why have they called us here?"

I sat in the chair opposite Sinnerman's grandmother and just looked at her for a moment. I suddenly didn't want to be the one to tell her any longer. I wanted to be anywhere but sitting in front of her. But I'd asked for this, and they were watching. There was no other choice now; I had to do it.

I took one of her hands and wrapped my fingers around it. "It's about your grandson," I said.

Her eyes lit up like she'd just screwed a shiny new light bulb into a dim-lit light.

"What—have they located him at last? Please tell me you've found him. But if we're here, it must be something bad. Oh no, is he dead?" She retracted her hand from mine and thrust both of them toward her face and flicked her head back and forth. "Please tell me he's not dead."

"I believe he's alive and well," I said.

Or alive anyway—"well" wasn't the best word choice for someone with his degree of instability.

She pulled her hands from her face and relaxed a little.

"Thank goodness. And I'm sure we owe it all to you. Tell me where he is—can we see him?"

"I don't know where he is," I said.

"What do you mean? I thought—"

"It's so hard for me to tell you this, but I wanted you to hear it from me."

"I can see it in your face," she said, "and in your eyes. What is it?"

"The day I was at your house, I took something from Samuel's room."

"What—why?"

"There was a notebook he'd kept wedged between the bed and the dresser, and I wanted to read it."

"You should have said something."

We were way past all that now. I leaned in closer.

"The writing in the book matched up with some of the notes your grandson sent me. How much do you know about the Sinnerman murders?"

"You mean the person responsible for the lives of all those women?"

I nodded.

"I just know what I've read in the papers," she said, "or saw on the news."

"We have a lead on a suspect and believe we know who he is."

"That's great, but why are you telling me all this, dear?"

I took a deep breath. *Slow and steady, you can do this.*

"The man, Sinnerman—he's your grandson."

Her eyes glazed over liked she'd just won the lottery, only when she arrived to claim her millions, she didn't have the numbers right.

She spoke, but not to me—to the air around her.

"This can't be, not my Samuel, surely they're mistaken. He's a good boy. He's had his problems like every other boy, but this? No, I don't believe it. Not a word of it. You're wrong. You have to be."

"Please, I know this is a lot to take in, but I wouldn't have ever told you if I wasn't sure. And believe me when I say I'm sorry." I placed my hand on her wrist. "I'm so sorry."

She was silent for a time during which her face changed from a soft pink to dull and ashen, like the life had been sucked out of her.

"When you were at my house, you said you thought my grandson knew your sister—that he was the last person to see her alive," she said.

I nodded.

"How did she die?"

It was the question I hoped she wouldn't ask, but she had every right to know the answer.

"I'm sure this has been hard on you. I don't want to make it worse."

"You can't say that to an old woman," she said. "Not after all this."

"All right then. My sister was murdered. She was the last woman killed in the first series of attacks a few years ago."

"And you believe my grandson did it?"

Up until now I'd looked her in the eye, faced her, and told her the truth. I thought about the pain I'd already caused, and I couldn't do it any longer. My eyes were so filled with liquid I couldn't see her properly if I tried. I looked away.

A few seconds went by, and we both remained silent. I felt her hand slip from mine, and when I turned back around, her eyes weren't open anymore, and she'd slumped down in her chair. I reached over and felt for a pulse—it wasn't there. I raced to the door but Coop had already witnessed the moment through the mirrored glass, and he flung the door open. He looked at the woman and then to me and said, "Way to go, Sloane. Nice job."

CHAPTER 53

Samuel's grandmother was transported to the hospital. She'd suffered a heart attack but was expected to get through it. I felt responsible. I needed to get out, to breathe. I put on my Band of Horses playlist on my iPod, which Maddie called my "sad music" even though I disagreed, and drove to the one place I felt a connection to family.

The cemetery was quiet as usual with all its residents engaged in their eternal sleep. Some of the stones cast shadows on the grass around them. I found Gabby's grave and positioned my body in front of it and sat down. I grasped both sides of her headstone with my hands, buried my head in the center, opened my mouth and let the words flow out of me.

"I wish I could talk to you, Gabby—even if for a single moment. I wonder if you're alive somewhere, living in peace in some type of afterlife, and if you're happy. I've spent the last few years thinking only of you, and I don't think I can do it anymore. I haven't felt like myself in such a long time, and I need to move on, live my own life. I know that now. But what I don't comprehend is how to do it. Here's my promise to you: I'm going to find Samuel Reids, the person who did this to you, and then I'm going to start my life all over again. You'll always reside in my heart, and I won't let a day go by that I won't think of you. But it's time for me to let you go and for you to do the same, and maybe both of us will find a sense of peace."

Once I'd finished, I returned to my car. The slight chill that came with the tail end of August swept past me and reminded me it was almost long-sleeve season again. Something moved in the tree next to me, and I halted and pulled my gun from its holster on my hip.

"Is anyone there?" I said.

No reply. Then the noise came again, above me. It shuffled and was restless, like the rustling of the trees in the winter wind. I pointed my gun toward the sky. An owl spread its wings and took flight.

I'd been on edge for weeks, and I needed to remember to take a breath every now and then. Giovanni's men had my back. I was safe, and everything was going to be all right. I slipped my gun back into its holster, unlocked my car door, and got in. I slid my key into the ignition and started the car.

"How touching. Did you tell your sister 'hi' from me?"

It was like time had slowed to a halt. I swung my head around and focused on the needle pressed against my neck. It was filled with fluid. One wrong move and it would pierce my skin.

"I've waited a long time for this."

"Me too," I said, "and I'm not alone."

"Correction: you weren't alone. I've taken care of the others. It's just you and me now. Feels good, doesn't it?"

I didn't know whether to believe him or not, but since no one had come to save me, I could only assume it was true.

"Why bother hiding yourself under a hat?" I said. "I know who you are, Samuel."

"Samuel's dead. It's Sam, or Sinnerman. Whichever you prefer."

I closed my eyes and tried not to lose myself to him. If I could just remain in control of the situation, even though it seemed like I was far from it at the moment, I might be able to save myself.

"Well, Sam, you should know your grandmother is in the hospital right now fighting for her life. She still cares about you."

He leaned in close, and I didn't know whether he was going to stick me or bite me. With each word, he uttered from his mouth, my neck felt more and more like it was on fire. I wanted to grab my gun, but I couldn't reach it unless I shifted my body toward the needle. It was too risky—I needed to wait.

"Don't waste your precious words on a family I no longer have or care about. I'm here to talk about you Sloane Monroe—about us.

Us? Was that his twisted fantasy—not to kill me at all? Had he imagined we could have some sort of life together?

"I'm here, now what?" I said.

"Drive."

"Where?"

"Let's take it one street at a time, shall we? Wave goodbye to your sister and then back out and make a right at the stop sign."

I reversed the car and turned right. Sam made a sound like the ticking of a clock and said, "Shame, shame. Not waving to your own sister. All this time, I thought she meant more to you."

"I left your grandmother out of it, now you extend me the same courtesy," I said.

"See how much we're alike, Sloane?"

"I'm nothing like you."

"Oh, but you are. Aren't you interested in how I know? I've watched you. Yes, that's right. Don't look so alarmed. At work, at home, out with your friends. I've been there, and I know everything. So much more than *they* know. Do you really think your friends know the real Sloane? Well," he whispered in my ear, "would it surprise you to find out they don't?"

"Why are you so interested in me?" I said.

He inched back from me but remained close and said, "Make a left at the next light."

"I asked you a question."

"You're in no position to make demands, but okay—I'll bite. At first I was intrigued by the resemblance between you and your sister. Oops—I forgot, no talking about sis. I followed you, I watched you put the board up in your office and then cover it so no one else could see. It was like our little secret. You returned to it time and time again and posted all the things you collected about me: the newspaper articles, the photos, and then the note I wrote you. They were all there on one beautiful board. I became the center of your life—you cared about me like no one else ever had."

Cared about him? He was more delusional than I thought, and I didn't know whether to play into his emotions or balk at them. The fear was gone, and my thoughts didn't center around what was to become of my life anymore. I was angry.

"Don't want to join the conversation?" he said. "That's okay; we have plenty of time."

"What did you do to the others?"

"Those men who followed you like lost lambs? I put

them to sleep."

"You didn't kill them?" I said.

"They are of no interest to me. Why would I bother?"

I felt a sense of relief and hoped he spoke the truth. I didn't want anyone else to die because of me.

"There is the matter of that boyfriend of yours we'll have to deal with."

"What do you mean?" I said.

"You'll have to tell him it's over so we can be together."

"I won't."

He was in my ear again. "So defiant. So different than the others. I like it!"

And I'd like it if he rotted into the fabric of the depths of hell.

"Take the next left please," he said.

I may have been showered in darkness, but I knew what part of Park City we were in and the neighborhood. Decklan's

My phone vibrated.

"Who would call at this hour? It's late, and you need your rest," he said.

I reached for it.

"You're not going to get that are you? Pass it back to me. And don't be foolish or try to be brave, or this needle goes all the way in."

I handed the phone back, and he pressed the flashing

green light on my screen.

"Sam Reids here, who am I speaking with?"

Someone responded and Sam said, "Sloane can't come to the phone right now. What's that? Oh, it's you— the soon-to-be ex-boyfriend. We were just talking about you. Tell me, were your ears ringing?"

The noise coming from the other end of the phone grew louder.

"Do not speak to me in that tone," Sam said, and then a moment later, "I'm afraid I'm going to have to cut this call short. I'm sure you understand. Sloane's with me now, so you can just go back to your life of petty crime and find someone else."

Another pause.

"Anger won't help you. Nothing will. You've lost her. Deal with it."

Inside my head, I had a *screw this* moment. My mind flashed back to a class on self-defense I'd taken the year before. The instructor said if I was ever abducted the best thing I could do was not to let the abductor reach their final destination and instead to ram the car into another car—this was supposedly the best option for survival. There were no cars on the street for me to plummet into so I sized up my only option and headed straight for it.

CHAPTER 54

I woke to find one of my wrists chained to a metal bar on the side of a bed. The other wrist was unrestrained, which confused me. Why would he allow me a small bit of freedom? My plan had failed, and no one knew my location, I was sure of it. I looked around. The room was decorated in the same colors and style as my room at home. Even the furniture was the same. The desk had several pictures on it of me with friends, family, and one with Sam. He'd cut out a photo of himself and stuck it next to my head to make it look like we'd posed for the photo together. To say he was out of his mind no longer applied—he was far worse than I imagined.

I lay still on the bed and tried to figure out my next move. Did I even have one? I had no idea how long I'd been out: an hour, several hours, days?

I heard something. At first it sounded like a wounded dog, but the more I listened the clearer it became. It was a person—a woman, and she was crying.

"Hello," I whispered. "Can you hear me?"

Silence. And then more whimpering.

"Who's out there?"

After another pause, the voice said, "Who are you?"

"My name is Sloane. What's yours?"

"Angela."

"How long have you been here?" I said.

"I—I don't know. I just want to go home."

"I'm going to do everything I can to make that happen."

"You can't. He's going to kill both of us."

"Angela, listen to me. I need you to tell me what you can see."

"I can't."

"Yes, you can. Just try. Anything you can tell me will help."

"No, I mean I really can't. There's a blindfold over my eyes."

A door opened and footsteps descended the stairs.

"Be quiet," Angela said. "Don't speak to him or he'll cut you—he doesn't like it when we talk."

Finally I understood why some of the women had cuts on their legs. Maybe one gash was administered each time they spoke as a way to silence them. I didn't care—I wasn't about to keep my trap shut.

Sam walked into the room and sat at a desk across

from me.

"Sorry about the handcuffs," he said. "Or should I say cuff. I didn't want to restrain you, but we need to have some kind of understanding."

"Like what?"

"No more running cars into trees and trying to hurt yourself. I need to be able to trust you."

I couldn't believe he thought I was trying to hurt *myself.*

"Why is the room decorated like this?"

"It's our room, Sloane. Don't you like it?" he said.

Every time he said my name, I wanted to projectile vomit all over him.

"I'll admit, at first when I followed you I was just going to kill you. But over time I developed feelings. I wouldn't say love—after all, what is love, really? And what do people mean when they say they're *in love.* Do they even know what they're saying? What we have is more real than any kind of simple love. We admire each other. Me from afar watching you, and you stopping at nothing to find me. I'm meant to have you. Wouldn't you agree?"

At some point, his fantasies convinced him that we shared the same obsessions.

"You're insane if you think any type of love exists between us," I said.

His voice elevated.

"You have a naughty mouth, and you need to get control of what comes out of it, or I'll have to cover it up, and then you won't be able to talk at all. Don't you treat me like you don't want to be here, after all I've done for us."

I wanted to fight, to tell him how much he reviled me—but I knew I'd said too much already.

"Tell me about my sister," I said.

"Now you want to talk about her?"

"You were the last one to see her alive. When she spoke her last words, only you were there to hear them."

"All right then," he said.

There was one thing Sam didn't know about me. I had small hands and even smaller wrists, and he hadn't put the cuffs on tight enough—I could feel it. While he blabbed on, I twisted and turned my wrist. I didn't care if I broke every bone in my body—one way or another, I would free myself.

Sam continued, "Your sister, as you know, was the last of my first victims, so she had to be the most beautiful. And she was—spectacular, just like you. I met her at the gas station. She asked if she could bum a cigarette from me. And I told her I didn't smoke, but I went in the store and bought her a pack, and she was so thrilled she didn't think twice when I asked her to come over to my car so I could give her a light. You two may look alike, but she didn't possess half your brain." He shook his head. "No sir.

She pleaded and begged, and even when I cut her, she wouldn't stop the constant jabbering."

I felt my left eye go moist—I wanted to keep control of my emotions, but his callous words were too much.

"Wow," he said. "Fascinating. Most girls cry for themselves, for their own lives, and they'd do anything to spare it. Not you though. You shed a single tear, and it's for someone who's not even alive."

"I don't want to hear anymore."

"Even if she mentioned you?"

"What?"

"Just before I squeezed her life away she said she was sorry about how things ended when you last talked to each other." He laughed. "Of course she was talking to herself, but even so, I suppose that means something to you."

It meant everything. The last time I saw Gabby I was angry with her because she'd decided to marry a man she barely knew. I'd thought about that conversation over and over—if only I could have taken it all back.

"Why don't you let the girl in the next room go?" I said. "She doesn't deserve to be here."

"I'm offended by that, Sloane. I got her for *you*."

"I don't understand?"

"It took me months to find someone who looked like your best girlfriend. Madison, is it? No, that's not right. You call her Maddie. But finally I did, and now you'll have no reason to leave. You have me, and you have your friend, and you'll stay with me. And we can be together."

"It doesn't work like that," I said. "This isn't some silly little game; you can't keep me here."

"Of course I can."

"I'm not your mother, Sam. You can't create a world like this and think it's perfect and expect me to live in it with you. You can't keep me here against my will. Nothing you say to me will justify you killing innocent women you son of a bitch!"

Sam bolted out of the chair and grabbed the framed photographs and threw them into a trash can next to the door. Facing me, he balled his hands into fists and whacked both sides of his head with them.

"I hate you! Do you hear me? I wish you were dead! You were supposed to stay here and be with me and not leave. Why can't you do that? You don't care about anyone but yourself. You want to hurt me, and you want to leave me. Why? I did everything for you. I just wanted you to be happy, but you couldn't be that way with me, and that's why you went away. You left me."

He wasn't talking to me now. He was talking through me. He'd tapped into all his suppressed emotions and channeled his mother.

Sam crunched his fingers inward and reached for my neck. I finally broke free of the cuff and swung at his head as hard as I could. He flew backward and crashed into the wall. I ran out of the room and into the next, slamming and locking the door behind me. Angela lay still on the bed. Tears stained her cheeks. At least fifteen rows of gashes lined her legs, which made me wonder how long he'd kept her. I removed the blindfold, but I couldn't free her from the cuffs on her wrists and ankles.

When I looked into her eyes they reminded me of an animal who'd been severely beaten.

"Hang on, Angela. I'm going to get us both out of here."

"How?" she said.

Sam pounded on the outside of the door.

"You have no place to go, Sloane. Stay in there as long as you want. I'll be here when you come out."

"I'm scared," Angela said.

I searched the room.

"I need you to focus for me, okay? When he was in here with you, did you hear anything like where he might have got the knife he used or any other tools he kept in this room?"

The only answer she gave was in the form of mewling sounds.

"Angela! Do you want to get out of here or not?" I said.

"There's a drawer."

"That's good," I said.

I looked around and didn't see it.

"Where is it?"

"Under my bed."

I got down on all fours and looked, but it was too dark. I took my hand and stretched it out as far as it would go, and then I felt something. I pulled out two boxes. One contained several knives in different shapes and sizes…and in the other was one item: my gun. I checked it. Still loaded.

I looked at Angela, "Be right back."

I turned the knob on the door and peered out with my gun aimed and ready. But I wasn't the only one. Sam lunged at me, knife in hand and slashed my arm. Blood sprayed out, and my gun crashed to the floor. Sam went for it, but I was ahead of him. I kicked his legs out from under him, and he tumbled and fell. I recovered my gun and pressed it against his chest.

"Go ahead, do it," he said. "It's what you want to do. It's what you've always wanted to do. I see that now."

I wanted to fire my gun into his heartless body until no bullets remained—the time had come, I had my one wish in life: Sinnerman on the ground with me at the helm. Part of me wanted to squeeze the trigger, but instead I took my free hand and yanked the cuffs from my pocket.

"Put them on," I said.

He stared at me, speechless.

"Do it!" I said.

He cinched them around his wrists, and I made a fist and hit him with everything I had inside me, again and again. Three years of fury expelled from my body. I released all of my pent up emotions on him and let the tears run free.

Blood oozed from Sam's face and covered my hands, now sheathed in red. A hand touched my shoulder, and I swung around.

"That's enough, cara mia."

I looked up into familiar, dark eyes.

"How did you find—"

"GPS sensor under your car."

I looked down at Sam and aimed my gun at his heart. His body was still and lifeless.

"I need to do this, Giovanni. He has to pay."

He shook his head, and gently reached for my hands, wiping some of the blood off with his sleeve.

"You found him, just like you wanted. Killing him won't make you feel any better. Trust me."

I nodded.

"There's another girl here. I need to help her."

"Go take care of her," he said. "I'll stay with him."

I walked toward Angela's room. Sam raised his head off the ground and muttered, "Sloane, don't leave me."

Giovanni replied, "Looks like I just got her back. Deal with it."

Two shots were fired, but I didn't turn around. I didn't have to; I knew it was all over.

CHAPTER 55

"Talk about your knight in shining armor," Maddie said with a wink.

"I guess so. But it's over now. He's done his good deed for me and now he can go back to his life."

"That's what you want?"

"Maybe it's what he wants."

"He's smitten. Why would he want to leave now?"

"It's hard to say where we'll go from here," I said. "I'm not even sure how to go about it."

We embraced, and I stepped on the plane.

"Take good care of Boo for me," I said. "See you both tomorrow."

Maddie took Lord Berkeley's paw and waved it up and down in the air. "Say goodbye to your mommy. Time for us two to have some fun."

*****

The warm breeze of Baltimore, Maryland, drifted across

my face like a blanket just out of the dryer as I descended the stairs of Giovanni's private jet. It felt good to be free of bodyguards, Nick, and the plague Sinnerman inflicted on me over the past few years of my life. It felt like I'd carried the weight of many lives around, and now I was so light I needed to brace myself against something, so I didn't get swept away into the air.

I rented a car and used my cell phone to map my location. Twenty-three miles later, I arrived at my destination and parked in front of a powder-blue, single-wide trailer with what used to be white trim. Now it held a kind of brownish hue. The trailer looked like it had been moved more than its share of times in its lifetime.

The door was the color of a fire engine, except duller, and on one of the single-pane windows in the front someone had taken their finger and scratched the word "hi" in the caked up layer of dust. Grass had been planted in the yard at one time, but had long since gone, leaving small patches of yellow about the size of a plate in its wake. A single car was parked out front; a purple Saturn sedan circa 1993 or so.

I ascended the two-by-four, wood-planked stairs and knocked.

A woman with a face that resembled the back of my elbows answered the door in a tattered peach robe and long, stringy hair. The distinct smell of gin floated by and was absorbed into the atmosphere.

"Can't you read?" she said and pointed to the sign that was hot glued to the door. "No solicitors. That means you, missy."

I spread out my fingers.

"Do you see me carrying anything?"

"Well, no."

"What does that tell you then?" I said.

"You've got a sharp tongue, anyone ever tell you that?"

"Can we skip the small talk and get to why I'm here?" I said.

"Patience isn't your strong suit, I guess."

Not even one minute with the woman, and I already wanted to wring her neck.

"Do you have a son named Sam—I mean, Samuel Reids?"

She looked like the ghost of her dearly departed grandmother had just appeared before her and said "BOO."

"Has something happened—is he dead? Did he leave money for me in his will? I just knew that boy would grow up and still find a way to care for his mama."

She spread the door all the way open, smiled and said, "Won't you please come in?"

Under any other circumstances I would have protested based on the smell alone, but I'd come too far to turn back.

She reached down and picked up a variety of plates, silverware, and other items on the sofa. "Sit, sit," she said.

"I'm not here about his will."

She scrunched up her face and frowned and said, "Oh, hmm. He hasn't gone and gotten you pregnant has he, because if you all need a place to stay, it's not here. There's no room at the inn."

A man emerged from the hallway wearing a stained, yellow shirt. His legs were almost all the way exposed except for a pair of boxer shorts, and his hair looked like it hadn't been brushed for days. He passed by Laurel who stood next to the bar in the kitchen and smacked her on the ass.

"Why would he ever want anything from you after what you put him through?" I said.

She flashed me a dirty look and said, "You did not just say that to me."

"Who you talkin' about?" the man said.

"Leave it alone, Larry," Laurel said.

On a scale of one to leave it alone, I wasn't about to let it go.

"I flew here to talk about your son, and no, I'm not pregnant with his child, and he doesn't need a place to live. He has one: permanent residence at the Park City Cemetery."

"My son's where? What—"

Larry looked at Laurel and said, "You have a kid?"

Laurel turned to him.

"Yes—I mean no—I mean—I used to."

"How in the hell do you used to have a kid?"

"It's not what you think."

"I don't think nuthin'. I'm outta here," he said. He walked out the door, got into the Saturn, and left.

"Guess he's not going to get dressed first," I said.

Laurel turned toward me.

"You're ruining my life. Just leave—please!"

I shook my head and laughed.

"It's still all about you, isn't it? After all these years. You just don't get it. You sit here in your piece of shit trailer and don't even have a clue what you've missed out on."

"I've lived a full life."

"Do you even care what your son did?"

"Should I?"

"Ever hear about the Sinnerman murders?" I said.

She tilted her head to the side like she was in deep thought, which seemed like a stretch.

"Seems like I did hear something about that a few years ago. Happened in Park City, right?"

"In your son's house, actually."

"I can't believe he'd ever live with anyone capable of committing murder."

"He didn't," I said.

"Well then…"

I gave it a moment to let it sink in, and then another, until it got to the point that I was going to have to get a chalkboard out and draw a diagram for her. I spoke in a slow and distinct manner. "Your son is the Sinnerman killer. He murdered many women, including my sister. And now he's paid with his own life."

"But how—"

I shook my head.

"Right now, I talk and you listen."

Her jaw popped open like no one had ever spoken to her that way before. Maybe if they had, she wouldn't have turned out to be such a waste.

"When your son was just a boy, you knew he had problems. Maybe a little anger inside, maybe he didn't develop the same as the other kids, but something was different. And you chose to turn your back on him. I'm here to tell you what happened after that," I said. "His own father couldn't look at him without thinking of you, so he sent him away to school, and then when he was a teenager, he kicked him out and left him on his own to fend for himself. At some point he fantasized about killing women and then one day he did. And do you want to know who those women looked like? You."

I stood up and walked to the door and opened it. "You're a horrid wretch of a woman, and I just wanted to come here and say that to your face."

CHAPTER 56

It felt good to touch down in Salt Lake City. I was home, and my life had taken on new meaning. I didn't know the course my new life would take, but I knew one thing: I would always take the time to appreciate the people in my life, and I'd spend the rest of it living for me and partaking in all that life had to offer. That's what Gabby would have wanted.

When the door to the plane opened, I was greeted by Maddie, Giovanni, and an exuberant Lord Berkeley, who scraped at my ankles until I bent down and lifted him up. Maddie opened the car door and pulled out a martini which she offered me.

"What's the occasion?" I said.

"You are."

I sniffed the glass.

"This is exactly what I need right now."

"Only the best for my best pal. And besides, I know

it's your favorite."

Maddie and Giovanni exchanged glances.

"What's going on with you two?" I said.

She reached out her hands and snatched Lord Berkeley from me and then turned and took him to the car. She reemerged with a suitcase.

"Uh, Maddie," I said. "What's this?"

"Giovanni called me yesterday and asked how I felt about him borrowing my friend for a few days," Maddie said.

"You're kidding me, right?" I said.

"Have you ever been to Italy?" he said.

"I don't know what to say, I mean—I just got here," I said.

"Say yes, ya dingbat," Maddie said. "Have fun you two."

A man came around the side and loaded my bag onto the plane.

"Well," Maddie said, "me and the Boo-ster here are off to get some dog treats. You guys have a good time, and buy me something good!"

Once she was gone and we were surrounded on all sides with hazel-blue skies, Giovanni reached over and pulled me into him and said, "I've wanted to do this since the moment we met." This time when my eyes closed and he leaned in, our lips found a connection. It was like being kissed for the first time. And yes, it was *first-prize-at-the-fair* good.

*****

Please feel free to let Cheryl know what you thought of Murder in Mind.

FOR UPDATES ON
CHERYL AND HER BOOKS

Blog: cherylbradshawbooks.blogspot.com

Web: cherylbradshaw.com

Facebook: Cheryl Bradshaw Books

Twitter: @cherylbradshaw

ALSO BY CHERYL BRADSHAW
Black Diamond Death (Sloane Monroe Series #1)

I Have a Secret (Sloane Monroe Series #3)

Sloane Monroe Series Boxed Set (Books 1-3)

Whispers of Murder (A Novella)

*The first chapters of all Cheryl Bradshaw's books
can be read on her blog*

Made in the USA
Las Vegas, NV
19 September 2023